P9-DNL-235

SUSPICION AT SEVEN

SUSPICION AT SEVEN

ANN PURSER

BERKLEY PRIME CRIME, NEW YORK

THE BERKLEY PUBLISHING GROUP
Published by the Penguin Group
Penguin Group (USA) LLC
375 Hudson Street, New York, New York 10014

USA • Canada • UK • Ireland • Australia • New Zealand • India • South Africa • China

penguin.com

A Penguin Random House Company

Berkley Prime Crime Books are published by The Berkley Publishing Group.
BERKLEY® PRIME CRIME and the PRIME CRIME logo are trademarks of
Penguin Group (USA) LLC.

Library of Congress Cataloging-in-Publication Data

Purser, Ann.
Suspicion at seven / Ann Purser.—First edition.
pages ; cm.—(Lois meade mystery ; 7)
ISBN 978-0-425-26178-1 (hardcover)
1. Meade, Lois (Fictitious character)—Fiction.   2. Murder—Investigation—Fiction.
3. England—Fiction.   I. Title.
PR6066.U758S87 2014
823'.914—dc23
2014031990

FIRST EDITION: December 2014

PRINTED IN THE UNITED STATES OF AMERICA

10   9   8   7   6   5   4   3   2   1

Cover illustration by Griesbach/Martucci.
Cover design by George Long.

Grateful thanks to Sally, who grew up in a bakehouse, and has many wonderful memories, and to Lydia, who is an expert on many things including pyramid selling.

SUSPICION AT SEVEN

ONE

ᔔ

Lois Meade, businesswoman and unpaid amateur detective, sat on the low wall of the millpond and watched the flow of water in the tailrace, where ducks and drakes were flapping about in the antics of courtship. It was spring, and love was in the air. Oddly enough, murder was also in the air.

Murder in Brigham, a small picturesque village, was shocking for all its inhabitants, and especially those near to the scene of the crime, the Mill House Hotel, a beautiful restoration of the old mill house and working machinery.

Lois, living in nearby Long Farnden, was particularly concerned, as her long-term interest was working with the legendary Inspector Hunter Cowgill in solving crime puzzles that took her fancy. She and Cowgill had a good working relationship, and though Cowgill was smitten long ago with her lovely smile, sharp tongue and long and shapely legs, Lois kept him at a suitable distance with ease.

Occasionally, Cowgill would wonder what he would do if Lois returned his passion, but acknowledged to himself that common sense would prevail and it would be he who backed off.

Lois was happily married, had three grown-up offspring and ran her own cleaning service, nattily entitled New Brooms, with "We Sweep Cleaner" added on the side of her van. Now she looked over at Brigham Bakery, still with its old bread oven and flour bins lining the bakehouse walls. Here Aurora Black made bread with flour from the mill, and in the old way baked beautifully crusty loaves for sale to customers, some from the Mill House Hotel, and most to the locals who knew a good loaf when they tasted one.

She and Lois were good friends, both of an age and both successful businesswomen. New Brooms cleaned the bakery, and Lois bought all her bread from Aurora.

Aurora's husband, Donald, dealt in jewellery, costume jewellery of little value but plenty of sparkle, which he hawked around the country and sold in pyramid parties, including one or two a year in the Mill House Hotel.

Donald was small in stature and wore built-up shoes to give himself extra height. He was inordinately proud of his glossy black hair. Blacky had been his nickname at school, but, fortunately, he was stocky and strong, and could fight his corner with total success.

Aurora, now punishing a large crock full of bread dough, was a natural blonde, and several inches taller than Donald.

Being a sensitive soul, she did not possess a single pair of high-heeled stilettos in her entire wardrobe.

Her arms and hands were beautiful in the powerful action of kneading, and now, catching sight of Lois by the pond, she decided the dough had the necessary elasticity, and she put it aside to prove. "Bread Baked by Hand" was her shop's slogan, and as a result, her output was not huge. She had a long waiting list of potential customers wanting to join her orders list.

Lois, who was early for an appointment to see a new client for her cleaning business, walked across the road and into the bakery shop to say hello.

"Morning, Aurora," she said, kissing her floury cheek. "Any bread left?"

"Your usual, yep. Did you want extra?"

"If you've got a large stone-ground wholemeal, that would be great."

The bread was fresh out of the oven, still warm, and Lois resisted the temptation to break off a crust and eat it then and there.

"Donald doing all right?" she said, hoping Aurora would say he was out. She had never been able to like her friend's husband, finding him shifty, flirty and too anxious to please.

"Yes, thanks. He's got a jewellery party in your village next week. Six thirty in Farnden village hall. Spread the word." She pulled a small poster from under the counter. "Would your Josie put this up in her shop?"

"Natch," said Lois. "And how's your Milly? She must be nearing her finals, isn't she?"

Aurora nodded. "She's on the heart ward at the moment. All drama is there, according to her!"

"She's a lovely girl," said Lois. "Deserves to do well."

Milly was the only child of Donald and Aurora. She was small, with large brown eyes and an almost permanent smile for everyone. She had wanted to be a nurse since she was five, when Aurora had rummaged in the attic and found a nurse's uniform from her own childhood.

"She hopes to come home for a weekend very soon, so perhaps we'll come over and cadge a coffee. And what's new in Farnden?" said Aurora. "This village is buzzing with the latest here. A poor woman found dead in the bed in the hotel. Cause not yet known. A nasty business on our doorstep, and many of my customers are upset and nervous about what might happen next. Anyway, rumour is rife, as they say."

THE FRESH GREEN OF NEW LEAVES GLADDENS THE HEART, THOUGHT Lois, and as she drove home from Brigham, through dappled sunlight in tree-lined lanes, she thought how lucky she was to live here in the middle of England in a county as yet undiscovered by colonies of London commuters.

Long Farnden and Meade House were eight miles from Brigham, and Lois meant to call in at her daughter's village shop back home. Josie and her husband, Matthew, along with her brothers Douglas and Jamie, completed Lois's family, not forgetting her husband, Derek, and mother, Elsie "Gran" Weedon.

Meade House in Long Farnden had belonged to a village doctor, long since retired, and though the young ones had all flown the nest, Lois's mother, known by most as Gran, lived with them and regarded herself as indispensable to the running of the household.

"MORNING, MUM," SAID JOSIE, AS LOIS CLIMBED THE STEPS INTO the shop and picked up the local paper. "How's everything?"

"Everything's fine," said Lois. She handed over the flyer advertising the jewellery party. "Would you put this up for Aurora Black's husband? It's one of his bling parties."

"Bling, eh? What a modern mum!"

"What I really mean is sparkly rubbish. Still, I hope he does well for Aurora's sake." She did not add that Donald Black was a charmer who could sell his own grandmother, and had a reputation for using his away parties as excuse for carrying on with a pretty woman.

Lois opened out the newspaper and scanned the columns.

"What are you looking for?" said Josie.

"Something Aurora said this morning. Some woman apparently found dead in bed in the Mill House Hotel, opposite the bakery."

"And you thought it might be a juicy one for Lois Meade, private detective?"

Lois shrugged. "Who knows?" she said. "You might hear something from Matthew, anyway."

Cowgill's nephew, Matthew Vickers, a young policeman and Josie's new husband, had been useful to Cowgill on a number of cases.

"What's the woman called, or don't we know? Police making enquiries an' all that?" asked Josie.

Lois nodded. "Aurora didn't have any details, so I thought it might be in this week's local newspaper. Yes, look, here's something on it." She turned the paper round so that Josie behind the counter could also see it.

"'Woman dead in bed,'" read Josie. "Sounds like the title of a book. No, there's not much here. She arrived the day before, apparently. Why don't you ring Uncle Hunter and then we can all know the gory details from the horse's mouth?"

"You know perfectly well," said Lois stiffly, "that anything I learn from Inspector Hunter Cowgill about police work is strictly confidential. You know that from your Matthew. And anyway, she might have died from a stroke, or something equally innocent."

"Well said, Mum," said a deep voice at the open door of the shop. It was Douglas, Lois's firstborn, and a solid citizen of Tresham.

"Hi, Doug," said Josie, and Lois gave him a peck on the cheek. "What brings you to Farnden this morning?" she said.

"Oh, nothing much. I was on my way to Waltonby and thought I'd stop by and say hello."

"Come up to the house and have a coffee with me and Gran. Your father may still be at home." Derek was an electrician, and his own boss.

Douglas nodded, and as another two customers had arrived, Lois waved to Josie, shouted to her that Aurora and Milly might be over at the weekend, and started off with Douglas up the rise to Meade House.

Two

❧

GRAN, STANDING AT THE RAYBURN AND TESTING A CAKE with a skewer, saw Lois and Douglas go by the window and waved, delighted to see her grandson.

"Give your old gran a kiss then," she said, as they came into the kitchen. Douglas gave her an affectionate hug, and sat down at the large table.

"You staying for lunch, boy?" she said.

The three sat around the table and talked of family concerns for a while, and then Lois asked if Douglas had heard anything about the woman found dead in bed at the Mill House Hotel.

"Only what you mentioned in Josie's shop," Douglas said, and Gran shook her head.

Lois showed them the newspaper, and Gran tut-tutted. "Sounds like a crime of passion," she said. "Or she could have forgotten to take her pills," she added. "I know if I were sleeping in a strange bed, which, God forbid, I would be out of my usual routine and probably even forget to wash me face."

The phone rang, and Lois jumped up quickly to answer it in her office. New Brooms was a busy concern, and with six cleaners and at least forty regular clients, the office was a hive of activity.

"HELLO? WHO'S THAT?"

"Inspector Cowgill for you, Mrs. Meade. Just putting you through."

"Lois, my dear, how are you this bright day?"

"Fine, thanks. What do you want?"

Cowgill resisted the impulse to tell her that she was the thing he wanted most in the world, and said that he had a new case which might interest her. He would appreciate her help.

"That poor woman found dead in bed in the Mill House Hotel?"

"Exactly," said Cowgill. "It's not as bald and straightforward as it seemed at first. Could I call and have a talk?"

"Police business?"

"Of course, Lois dear. I'll be with you at five."

Lois put down the phone and smiled. Good old Cowgill. He was semiretired, but seemed to do as much as he always had. He had a terrific reputation with the force, and they were happy to keep him on. His nephew, Matthew, was rising through the ranks, but Cowgill was careful to avoid any suspicion of nepotism.

Back in the kitchen, where Gran had made coffee, Lois said it had been a New Brooms call, and she would be having a visitor this afternoon. She hoped to get to the front door before Gran, but it was a forlorn hope.

"A new client?" said Douglas.

"What visitor?" asked Gran.

"Oh, all right then. Not New Brooms. It's Inspector Cowgill, wanting to talk about that woman dead in bed at the Mill House Hotel. Now, let's change the subject. How's the tiddlers, Dougie?"

"Fine, Mum. They're good little chaps, and Susie knows how to handle them."

"Love 'em and leave 'em alone; that was my policy," said Gran.

"Mum! It was 'Spare the rod and spoil the child,' if I remember rightly!" said Lois.

"Must be off now," said Douglas, sensing an argument. "Let me know, Mum, if you need an assistant."

"She already has one, though God alone knows why she has to choose a batty old woman. Mrs. Tollervey-Jones, of all people!"

"I'm already used to batty old women," said Lois with a smile, and added she would see Douglas to his car and give her small white terrier, Jemima (aka Jeems), a bit of a walk.

"HELLO, UNCLE HUNTER! HOW CAN I HELP YOU?" JOSIE GREETED Matthew's inspector uncle with a peck on the cheek. "Business call, or an afternoon off and here to see the family?"

Cowgill looked at her, so like Lois and equally lovely.

"I'm here to see your mother, but couldn't pass without saying hello. And, of course, to ask if you've heard any useful talk in the shop."

"About the woman in the Mill House Hotel? Oh yes, most of the old tabs who congregate in here on pension day, they had plenty to say this morning. One of them said she was a high-class fancy woman who usually turns up with a man. The same man every time. But this time she was on her own."

"How did this woman know that?"

"Son works for the hotel, in the bar. You lot have already interviewed him, so I'm not telling you anything new. Though there was one other woman who said she thought she knew who the man was, though it was all highly confidential. She looked embarrassed, as if she wished she hadn't said anything."

"Can you give me names, Josie?"

"No, sorry. Not unless it is unavoidable. If it got around that I was a nark, my shop would be avoided like poison. Mum being your little helper is bad enough."

"And being married to a policeman?"

"And being married to a policeman."

THREE

GRAN HAD REFUSED MANY TIMES TO HAVE HER HEARING tested, claiming it was as good as the day she was born. Lois suspected she could be conveniently deaf at times and sharp as a button at others. She sighed, as no sooner had the bell begun to ring than there Gran was, opening the door and greeting Cowgill with distinct coolness.

"Ferretin'," as Lois's husband called her detective work, was steadfastly frowned on by both him and Gran. Derek considered she had enough to do with New Brooms without running around after criminals, some of whom could be dangerous, and Gran's objection was terse and to the point. "A woman's place is in the home," she would say, loudly and often.

Now Lois asked her kindly if she could rustle up coffee for the inspector, and shut the office door firmly.

"It's some time since we cleared up the last case. How have you been Lois? Is business good?" Cowgill smiled affectionately at her over her desk.

"Fine, thanks. New client at, guess where, Brigham. My friend Aurora Black runs a bakery near the Mill, and, as I am sure you know, we have talked about the sad case of an unexplained death in the hotel."

Cowgill nodded. "Right, well, this woman, who checked into the hotel as Sylvia Fountain, arrived at about three o'clock in the afternoon with an overnight bag and went up to her room. She did not appear in the dining room for supper, nor at breakfast. The cleaning staff reported that they could get no reply to knocking, and asked if they should use their room key to go in."

"What time was this?"

"Ten o'clockish. The cleaners do not always go round the rooms in the same order, so they weren't absolutely sure, but more or less ten o'clock. When they went in, two of them, they saw the woman, still under the duvet and asleep, or supposedly asleep. Then one of them said the woman seemed very still, so they gently pulled back the duvet and saw at once that she was not breathing. The rest you can imagine."

"Not completely. Was she wearing nightclothes?"

"Ah, still thinking laterally, Lois. No, she was wearing the clothes she arrived in. And the next odd thing is that her overnight bag contained no night things. No nightdress, toothbrush, nothing you would expect to find."

"What was in it, then?"

"Jewellery. Bags of it. And, I am assured, all of it worthless. Costume jewellery, I believe it used to be called."

"Oh God. Not jewellery." Lois had paled.

"I know, Lois my dear. Your friend Aurora's husband, Donald Black. First on our list of suspects, of course."

"But she didn't say anything about him being involved when I was over there."

"No, well, when we spoke to him he had a cast-iron alibi. He was up north, far north, attending a conference on business management. They vouched for his every move, including sleeping in a school dormitory requisitioned for the purpose."

"Oh, how convenient! And the big question: how did she die?"

"Strangled with a silver necklace."

"Blimey," said Lois, and she frowned as the door opened and Gran entered bearing a tray of coffee and home-baked biscuits.

"You all right, Lois?" she said, frowning. "You look like a ghost! What've you been saying to my daughter, Inspector?"

"Oh, I'm okay, Mum. Thanks for the coffee."

The inspector had jumped up to help, and now closed the door behind a scowling Gran.

"Sorry, Lois. I didn't mean to alarm you. But I am afraid that Donald Black is still under surveillance. I am not sure how much he has told his wife, but she must be aware."

"Poor Aurora. What a slimy toad he must be. Beats me how he fathered that lovely Milly."

"Don't jump to conclusions, Lois. As I said, his alibi is watertight. In fact, so much so, that it is in itself odd, to say the least. Most of us cannot account for every minute of our day and night."

"Anything more to tell me?"

"Only that Miss Sylvia Fountain is known to us. Nothing serious. A little light shoplifting now and then. Also hires herself out to the highest bidder. Family money behind her, apparently."

"Where does she come from?"

"Variously at a number of addresses. Widowed aunt lives in relative luxury locally. Several brothers, who return to our notice on a regular basis. Small-time crooks, and not worth our time and trouble, mostly."

Lois did not reply for a minute, and then said that she presumed he wanted her to concentrate on the Brigham end of the case.

The inspector rose to his feet. "You know, my love, that whatever you decide to do is helpful to us. As long as you keep in touch and don't do anything foolish."

"Thanks, Cowgill. To be honest, I look at it like this. If I can help Aurora in any way, then I shall do so. And before you say it, I shall remember to keep mum on everything you've told me."

He laughed. "That's my girl," he said, and leaned across the desk to give her a light kiss. She did not push him away, but said, "You're allowed one. Being as you're family."

Four

❧

"DOUGLAS PHONED WHILE YOU WERE OUT WITH JEEMS," Derek said.

Lois had taken her dog to the nearby woods early, before breakfast. "She caught a rabbit," she said. "I've left it in the scullery for you to deal with. I was a bit cross with her, but as she killed it quickly, I thought we might as well not waste it. Mum loves rabbit."

"What's that Mum loves?" said Gran, coming into the kitchen.

Lois told her, and her long-suffering mother said that as long as Derek drew and skinned it, she'd make rabbit pie for tonight's supper.

"I might be out for supper," Lois said. "Aurora has asked me over to see some new stuff Donald has for sale. She wants me to stay for supper. Perhaps we could have rabbit pie tomorrow?"

Gran sniffed. "You don't fool me, Lois Meade," she said. "You're ferretin' again. To do with that strangled tart, I suppose."

Lois did not deny this, but said Josie's birthday was coming up, and Donald Black had got some new stuff to show her.

"I should think we could do better than that rubbish for our Josie's birthday," said Derek. "I suppose it is no good saying you'd do better to keep well away from Brigham and that latest case?"

"Who said anything about the latest case?" said Lois.

"Inspector Cowgill did," said Gran. "I just happened to be coming along with your coffee, and you know what a deep voice he has. It carries, you know."

"Mum! You were listening at the keyhole!"

"Of course I wasn't! How can you say such a thing to your own mother?"

"Oh well. I expect the full details will be in the local papers by now. But for heaven's sake, if you heard anything else, keep it to yourself. And in answer to you, Derek my love, I promise to keep well away from anything dangerous. I really want to help in this case for Aurora's sake."

"Haven't you forgotten something?" said Gran with a smirk.

"No. Don't think so."

"Your son Douglas phoned. Shouldn't you go and phone him back?"

"Oh Lor, okay, okay. I'll go into my office."

She went quickly into the cool, soothing quiet of her office and dialled her son.

"Hello? Mum here. Did you want me?"

"Just idle curiosity, Mother dear. Brigham Bakery is in the news today. Isn't that the Blacks, opposite the hotel where that woman has been found dead in bed? I thought you might have an ear to Mrs. Black? Aren't they Brooms clients?"

"And I get my bread from them. Delicious it is, too, and Aurora Black is a very nice person. I count her as a friend. As for knowing anything more about the strangled woman, apart from the fact that her name was Sylvia Fountain and her occupation prostitute, then I don't know anything."

"Fountain? An old and disreputable family here in Tresham, so the gossip goes. So possibly one for Inspector Cowgill and his brilliant sidekick, Mrs. Lois Meade? No, don't answer that. The Fountains are known to be rich, largely as a result of dodgy dealings. Best not to have anything to do with any of them. We all love you, Mum, and don't want to lose you. 'Nuff said! Bye for now."

LOIS SPENT THE DAY VISITING CLIENTS AND CHECKING OVER THE accounts with Hazel in the Tresham office. She thought of calling on Susie, Douglas's wife, but looked at her watch and decided the best thing would be to see if Cowgill was in his office and find out how much he knew about Tresham's underworld in general and the Fountains in particular. He had spent a working lifetime in the area and probably knew all the villains, really bad, not so bad, and totally ineffectual.

The Nimmos were another such family, and Dot Nimmo, a member of Lois's team and cleaner extraordinaire, had opted out, more or less, but inside knowledge had proved invaluable in the past.

"Afternoon, Mrs. Meade," said the sergeant on the reception desk. "The inspector is in his office. Would you like to go on up and give him a nice surprise?"

Inspector Cowgill's partiality for Lois Meade was well known in the police station, and Lois said certainly not, she would be glad if he would wipe that grin off his face and enquire if the inspector was free.

By the time she had climbed the stone steps to his office, he was standing at his door ready to welcome her.

"To what do I owe this visit, Mrs. Meade?" he said formally, and then as soon as his door was shut, gave her a hug and drew up a chair for her.

"It's simple really," she said. "I've been thinking about the families known to be involved in a network of crooks in this town and around. More as background information, really. Nimmos I know about, and now there's the Fountains?"

The next half hour Lois listened carefully as Cowgill gave her information about people she had never met. The Nimmos seemed to have been a bunch of Robin Hoods, stealing from the rich to give to the poor, with no record of violence. Not so the Fountains. Mugging old ladies for their purses was a specialty.

"So what are you going to do? And is there anything I can be doing to make life easier for Aurora Black?"

"Trust me. I am sure you will be supporting her, and that is most important at the moment. She is carrying on with the bakery, and I suspect helping her is what you can do best. Now, Lois dear, unfortunately, much as I would love to keep you here for longer, I have a meeting to go to in five minutes. How's the family? Matthew and Josie seem blissfully happy."

"And why not? Anyway, I have to go now. Work to do. Oh, and by the way, when you come to see me in my office, keep your voice down. Mrs. Weedon, alias Gran, has super-efficient hearing."

FIVE

THE BLACKS LIVED IN THE REAR OF THEIR BAKERY, IN AN extension they had added years ago, when Aurora decided to set up her bread business in Brigham. They had one very precious child then, and had subsequently tried hard for another to be a companion for her.

Aurora had sadly given up the possibility of it happening by chance, and had secretly investigated the possibilities of success.

Although she did not want to blame Donald, she was pretty sure the fault was with him.

Now it was too late, and in any case, she had a business that required all her time, and as Donald was away frequently at his jewellery parties, she accepted that her life was full enough, and having Milly was a bonus.

She was expecting Lois Meade for supper, and Lois was

sure to be full of news of her children and grandchildren, just as it should be. She thanked God, not for the first time, that she had her wonderful daughter, Milly, and had been delighted to hear from her that she hoped to be with them tomorrow for a lightning visit.

"HI, LOIS, COME ON IN. SUPPER WON'T BE LONG, AND DONALD has made some Pimms for us. It is really summery today, isn't it? I must say you are looking very smart this evening. Don't know how you do it . . ."

"What with running a business, having children and grandchildren and keeping Gran happy? Are you thinking on those lines? Then you're absolutely right, and it is really nice of you to say so." Lois kissed Aurora on her cheek, and accepted a glass from Donald with a cool nod.

"Shall we have supper first, and then Donald can show you his latest collection? I must say I am tempted myself!"

What a pleasant couple, Lois thought to herself. Maybe I'm wrong about Donald. They seem so well adjusted to each other. None of the arguments that were a daily occurrence at Meade House. She watched as Aurora laid the table for supper, and Donald drew the cork from a bottle of red wine. She thought of Derek, who would be happy with a ham sandwich and a can of light ale.

But then she remembered how much her family actually enjoyed a good argument, a fierce battle of words without giving any quarter.

Perhaps Aurora, who was lively minded and good company, did not find Donald boring, with nothing to talk about but brooches, bracelets and necklaces. Baubles, bangles and beads!

They all helped with clearing the table, and then he produced his collection. Everything sparkled and shone. Lois had to admit that some of it was really attractive, and she picked up a delicate silver necklace with a single pearl drop.

"You could try it on, if you like," said Donald, and he walked round to fix the clasp at the back of her neck. The pearl nestled between her breasts, and she decided it would be foolish not to buy such a pretty thing. If Josie didn't like it, she would have it herself.

"How much does it cost?" she asked.

"Trade price to you, Lois. We never know when we might have to call on your New Brooms services to us at a revised special rate! We sole traders must stick together."

"That's the last one of those necklaces," said Aurora.

"Shouldn't you keep it for the collection? I am sure there's one with a blue stone set in faux diamonds that would suit Josie's colouring," Lois said.

"No problem. I can easily order another pearl one," said Donald. "It looks so good on you, Lois. Simple and elegant. You must have this one, dear." He found a box, and the necklace was safe in Lois's handbag. "Now, how about a pair of matching earrings?"

Lois laughed. "Sorry, no more pocket money this week. I think earrings would be overdoing it, anyway. Thanks, Donald. I shall enjoy this, either on Josie or myself!"

"Shall we have coffee now?" said Aurora, disappearing into the kitchen.

As soon as she had gone, Donald drew up a chair next to

Lois's and spoke in a whisper. "She's very upset by the murder in the hotel. The woman had some of my stuff in her bag. Not a direct seller, thank God. No, Aurora's not quite herself. I expect you've noticed? We're so glad Milly's coming tomorrow. It'll take her mind off it."

"Well, natural enough, I should have thought," said Lois. "You being taken in for questioning, an' that."

Donald shook his head. "I was hardly in the police station five minutes before they let me go. Watertight alibi, you see. And I'm not a liar, Lois. All true, and I have proof that I was up north all the time. Can you help me cheer her up? She's very fond of you."

At this point, Aurora came back with a tray of coffee and set it down on the table. "What are you two whispering about?" she said lightly.

"Cooking up a surprise birthday party for Lois," said Donald.

"Now it won't be a surprise," Aurora said, and ruffled his dark hair.

"Oh, yes, it will," he said, smoothing it back again. "Black or white coffee, Lois?"

Six

❧

NEXT MORNING, THE NECKLACE WAS EXAMINED BY GRAN and Derek, and pronounced very pretty and just the thing for Josie's birthday. "I'll get you another one, me duck," said Derek, seeing Lois's face. "That Donald Black, I'll have a word with him. He's coming over to the village hall, isn't he?"

"Now, how about this? It's Josie's birthday on Monday, so we can ask her and Matthew, if he's not on duty, to come over for a meal," Gran said.

"Oh, he'll be wanting to take her out for a treat, won't he? What do you think, Derek?"

"What about tomorrow lunch? We can tell her not to open the box until Monday."

"Fine," Lois said. "I have to go down to the shop, so I'll ask her then."

She went along to her office and set about sorting out her papers and schedules for the New Brooms meeting at twelve. She had rearranged the weekly meeting to be today instead of Monday, because of the birthdays. The girls and one young man would arrive in dribs and drabs, and then settle down to business. Lois's team was much as it was when she set up the cleaning agency some while ago. One or two had left, and others taken their place, but they were largely the same happy group who respected Lois and enjoyed the work they carried out for clients around the county.

Lois was born in Tresham on a council estate, where Gran and her husband had set up house, producing one beautiful girl. Gran always said that one like Lois was quite enough. Wayward and obstinate, refusing to knuckle down to schoolwork, Lois left when she was sixteen to work in Woolworths, where she caught the eye of the young electrician Derek Meade. He always said he courted her over the confectionary counter, and after a year or so going around together, they persuaded her mother and father to allow them to marry.

Mrs. Weedon knew that if they said no, the two would debunk to Gretna Green and get married anyway. So they agreed, and in no time young Douglas had come along, then Josie, and finally the concert pianist, Jamie. Sometimes Gran looked at him and wondered if he was a cuckoo in the nest. But no, he would always be Lois and Derek's baby, and success had not changed him. Nor had he tried to shove the others out! At times like Christmas, when the whole family gathered together, it was as if they had never left home.

*   *   *

AT TWELVE SHARP, THE DOORBELL RANG, AND HAZEL, WHO managed the office in Tresham, was first to arrive. The rest came in a bunch, all except Dot Nimmo, who was always last. Dot was special to Lois, having not only shined up many a dusty house, but had also helped out with ferretin'.

Dot, who was the widow of a gang boss in Tresham, had connections with the underworld that proved to be valuable. She had lost both husband and son, and had gone downhill in her lonely terraced house up the street from New Brooms office. Finally, in an attempt to pull herself together, she had asked Lois for a job. Against all advice from Gran and other team members, Lois had agreed. Dot was brash, bossy and totally loyal, and would go through fire to rescue Lois in trouble.

The other team members were Floss, young and newly married; Sheila Stratford, comfortable wife of a retired farmer; and Andrew Young. Andrew ran his own interior-decorating business alongside New Brooms, and had no qualms about scrubbing floors or polishing silver.

After Lois had thanked them for coming along on a Saturday, one by one they went through the work schedules, and then Lois asked for any queries they might have.

"It's not to do with cleaning, really, Mrs. M," said Dot. "But I just wondered if you'd heard anything about the goings-on in Brigham? Every house I've been to this week, there's been someone talking about it. They all seem to think the jewellery bloke done it. And ain't he coming to do one of his parties here in the village hall? Nobody seems to know if it's safe to go along."

"What?" said Lois loudly. "Donald Black a mass murderer? I think with a roomful of feisty women he'd stand no chance. No, it is serious, I know, particularly for his wife. But he's totally innocent. A watertight alibi, apparently. So I think you can all relax and enjoy an evening among the diamonds."

"So who did do it?" said Sheila. "Any ideas, Mrs. M? My husband said he knew what he'd do with the poncey idiot."

"Oh dear," said Lois. "So he's been found guilty by the gossips, has he? I've met him, of course, as has Floss when she's cleaning there. I have always bought my bread from his wife's bakery. But I really think we should leave this to the police. Now, can we get on with reports from clients? Andrew, would you make a start?"

"My report is not unconnected with Dot's contribution," he said. "I've had a request from the Mill House Hotel to redecorate the entire interior of the bedroom wing. And after that, the dining room and reception."

"Wow! Well done, Andrew. You won't have much time for New Brooms work, will you?"

"Oh yes I will, Mrs. M. I explained that I divide my time working for you alongside interior decor. They said I could surely combine the two. We could prepare a schedule, they said, and as cleaners were always hard to come by, there'd be no shortage of work. I think they must have been anxious to get me, probably because I undercut other estimates for the decor work."

"More likely they recognised you as a good interior designer, Andrew. I'm very pleased for you. We'll get together when you're more familiar with how it will work out," said Lois. She was anxious not to lose Andrew, since some of

New Brooms clients, particular single lonely bachelors, could be difficult with her girls. If Andrew was not free, she usually sent in Dot Nimmo, who was a match for any over-attentive male client.

"I'm next," said Sheila. "All my clients are happy, I hope. Nothing's been said, anyway. There's been talk of the Mill House Hotel affair of course, but I've not encouraged gossip."

Dot made a face. Gossip was meat and drink to her, and she regarded it as an essential part of her job, regardless of what the others thought. It was one of the rules of Brooms that they did not gossip, but got on with their work. Ferretin' was different, Dot had decided.

Now she raised her eyebrows and said that she had only one client in Brigham, and she was deaf and nearly blind, and though a dear old soul, did not get about much and so did not mention the murder.

"It's odd, don't you think, the way we all assume it was murder?" said Floss. She was a sensible girl, not long married, whose parents and husband thought she was too talented to be a cleaner. She ignored their criticism, however, and explained that she loved the job. There was great satisfaction to be gained from leaving a tidy, sweet-smelling house behind her when she had finished. Clients were a varied lot, and always interesting.

"There was a small paragraph in the evening paper, saying she had been found strangled, so I suppose that clinches it," said Andrew. "Maybe when I start at the hotel, I shall hear more details."

"Keep your ears and eyes open," said Dot, and caught Lois's eye. "But don't gossip, Andrew; there's a good lad." Her wink was obvious to all present, and Lois was unusually pleased when, with a tap on the door, Gran brought in coffee.

THE NEWS OF ANDREW YOUNG'S COMMISSION HAD SPREAD quickly around the Mill's employees. Some were pleased, and claimed they had suggested refurbishment long ago. Others were depressed, foreseeing disruption everywhere, with rooms out of action and notices of wet paint in all the narrow corridors and stairs.

"I hope he leaves my reception until last," said an attractive blonde German girl, whose English was better than most, and who had a gift for making guests feel welcome the moment they entered the doors. "Then I shall take a holiday and leave it all to a temp."

SEVEN

NEXT MORNING, LOIS SLID OUT OF BED WITHOUT DISTURB-
ing Derek, and tiptoed to the window. The spring
sunshine had gone, and rain was lashing the daffodils. So
much for dancing daffodils, she thought. They look ready
to go into retreat. Never mind; a rainy Sunday would be a
good day for catching up on paperwork.

"Hey, missus," said Derek from the bed. "Haven't you
forgotten something?"

"What?"

"Happy birthday, gel! Come back to bed and celebrate."

Lois smiled. "Derek!" she said, and took a flying leap,
landing on top of her protesting husband.

"Careful! Don't spoil the surprise," he said, and put his
arms lightly around her.

*　　*　　*

When Josie had been on the way, Lois had really wanted to share her own birthday, and had very nearly got her wish. But her baby girl had waited one more day before emerging into a waiting family. As a result, Lois had never wanted to do much about her own celebration, avoiding upstaging her daughter. This had become a custom over the years, and now Lois had for the moment forgotten today was hers, though she knew the family had decided otherwise.

"Bacon's like crispy leather, eggs are rock hard and I don't mind one bit," said Gran, with unusual sweetness. "Never mind, you two. We're having a good lunch, as discussed, but not here. So don't fill up too much now."

Breakfast had been over for some time, and Douglas had rung to say they would all meet at the Mill House Hotel at twelve. A table had been booked, and Matthew and Josie had confirmed that they would be there.

"And you are forbidden to talk shop with the management," said Derek to Lois. "No sneaking off for a ferretin' meeting with the cleaners."

"No cleaners there on a Sunday, surely," Lois said. "Though I suppose they have to make up clean beds an' that when guests go and new ones come in. Weekend shifts, there'll be."

When it had sunk in that her surprise was lunch for all the family in a posh hotel, and not just any old hotel, but the Mill, her brain began to work overtime. Who actually found the woman who had died there? Might be a chance to have a chat.

"No, Lois, no! I can see from your face you are plotting something! If necessary, we shall manacle you to your chair."

"Don't worry, Derek; I'll behave," she said. "I think I'll go for a quick dog walk now. I can put on rain gear, and Jeems doesn't specially like getting wet, so we won't be long."

The rain had stopped now, but the woods were dripping. After the storm thrush's solo, birds had begun to sing again, and Lois strode purposefully through familiar footpaths. Farnden woods had once been a spinney, now overgrown, behind the big house where Lois's ferretin' assistant, Mrs. Tollervey-Jones, had lived for most of her life. She had moved into a smaller house in the village centre, only a few paces from the Meades. The new people had turned the whole estate into a moneymaking enterprise, and Lois averted her eyes from signposts along the path such as "Piglet's House" and "Hedgehog Hollow." She thought about Aurora Black, and wondered how she and Donald were coping, with him under such unjust local suspicion. The poor woman must be reluctant to face her customers, knowing what the gossips had been chewing over. With luck, seeing Milly again would do her a power of good. She wondered if Donald's jewellery parties would be affected. Fewer customers, perhaps. Or maybe a larger attendance of curious women. Safety in numbers, possibly?

"Penny for 'em, Mother-in-Law!" It was Matthew Vickers, Josie's husband and Cowgill's nephew, being pulled along by a very young and sprightly terrier of mixed origin.

"Matthew! What are you up to in these woods? Not on duty, I hope. Keeping an eye on Mrs. Tiggywinkle's ironing? Honestly, aren't these signposts awful! And how's the new pup? He's very sweet, and Jeems loves him. I know we're meeting you later at the Mill House Hotel and I'm really looking forward to it."

"So are we, and happy birthday to you. I love family get-togethers, and I know Uncle Hunter is delighted to be asked."

"Is he asked? Well, that's a turn up. Must be hands-off day for Derek and Gran, who are always pushing me to give up ferretin'."

"That was Derek's word, wasn't it? Should go into the policeman's standard dictionary."

"Better get on, then. We shall be wanting to look our best for the Mill House Hotel."

"You are always at your lovely best," said Matthew gallantly. "You know what they say. Always look at the cat before you look at the kitten. I did, and managed to snatch Josie from an unsuitable match."

"So, following that to its natural conclusion, do you think Derek took a good look at Gran before rescuing me from Woolworths?"

Matthew walked off, still laughing, and Lois continued on her way.

EIGHT

❧

INSPECTOR COWGILL WAS THE FIRST TO ARRIVE AT THE HOTEL, and on checking in, showed the receptionist his police badge and said he would like to have a wander around, if that would be convenient. "Not on duty, of course. This is a special birthday party for mother and daughter. But while I'm here, there are one or two things. I shall be as inconspicuous as possible."

The receptionist was smitten by his charm, and directed him to the restaurant as and when he was ready.

Next through the double doors was Jamie, with Douglas and Susie and the grandchildren, then Josie and Matthew and Gran, making up the whole party, except for Lois and Derek.

When they were all seated, Gran said there was an empty chair, and had the staff got the numbers wrong?

"No," said Josie. "That'll be for Uncle Hunter. He'll be

here in a minute. Reception said he was looking around for a short while."

"Cowgill?" said Derek, frowning. "What does he have to do with Lois's birthday?"

"He's family now, Dad," Josie said quietly. "Don't make a scene."

Derek subsided, muttering.

After much deliberation over the menu, all were finally served, and Derek, lifting his glass, called for a toast to Lois. "To my wife," he began, "mother and grandmother, the lovely and talented Lois Meade. And to my daughter, Josie, who had the good sense to marry a policeman, I ask you to raise your glasses. Happy birthday, Lois and Josie!"

He bent down and gave Lois a smacking kiss, and then sat down in a storm of clapping.

"Speech," cried Jamie, and all joined him. "Speech!"

Lois rose to her feet. "On behalf of me, and Josie tomorrow, thank you all for this lovely surprise," she said, "and especially Derek, who is no good at keeping secrets!" More clapping. "And also, I must say how pleased I am to see Uncle Hunter among us. Welcome, Hunter."

More clapping from all except Derek and Gran.

WHEN THEY WERE ON TO COFFEE AND CHOCOLATES, LOIS excused herself to go to the ladies' room. She left the dining room and asked a passing waiter to direct her. After she had freshened up, she left, and instead of going back to the restaurant, she turned in the opposite direction and headed for the bedroom wing. There was nobody around, and she had no idea which room had been the one where the unfortunate Fountain woman met her end.

"Can I help you?" a voice behind her said.

"Oh yes, I am a bit lost," said Lois. "I need to find my friend's room. I think she said it was the one next to the murder scene."

"Oh crumbs," said the cleaning girl. "I'll point you in the right direction."

After two fire doors, Lois came to a room with the familiar police tape still covering the entrance to number 12. The next room, Lois saw, was number 14.

"Superstitious?" she said quietly. She tested the tape, and found it was insecurely fastened. One quick tug, and it was free. She opened the door softly and tiptoed inside. There was nothing untoward to see. The bed had been stripped down to the mattress, the cupboards were empty, and in the small bathroom, everything shone, clean as a new pin

Hearing voices, Lois quickly looked around but could see nothing untoward. The voices were still in the distance, and she retreated, refixed the tape and walked purposefully back the way she had come. Once more she met the cleaning girl, who now was chatting to a workmate.

"Afraid my friend is out," Lois said cheerfully, as she passed, and in no time was back at the table with the others.

"Why don't we do that party thing, where we all change places and have someone new to talk to?" said Douglas. His children had vanished to play with another pair from a nearby table. They had been strictly warned not to go near the millpond or the streams running through and turning the great wheel. This had been renovated and spotlit, then

glassed in, so visitors could stand and watch safely, mes-
merised by the tipping buckets spilling water through the
channels and into the pond.

"Don't be a nuisance!" shouted Douglas. "And do what
the big girls tell you."

A waiter, hovering to take away dishes, said they shouldn't
worry; all the dangerous places had been made secure, and
no harm could come.

"I tell you what, Douglas," Lois said. "I'll go with them.
I'd love to explore a bit. Then I'll bring them back soon."

She followed where the children had gone, and found
them, noses pressed to the glass, staring at the slowly turning
mill wheel, dripping with yellowish-green weed.

Lois joined them. It was so beautiful in its peaceful progress, and yet in former days, it had turned great machinery
in the mill, powering it in its grinding of flour to make
bread, the staff of life. And now, in one of the hotel's small
anonymous bedrooms, a life had been taken away.

"DREAMING, LOIS?" IT WAS COWGILL, UNCLE HUNTER, AND HE
stood close to her, watching the wheel.

"No, not really. Are the others going? Better be going back
to say cheerio and thanks to my family. It's been a lovely treat.
Come on, kids. Back we go." She turned to Cowgill and said,
"I'm so glad you came, you old fraud."

They all left the Mill in excellent mood, Douglas and
family to go back to Tresham, Josie and Matthew with Uncle
Cowgill to their small cottage, and Jamie to return with
Derek, Lois and Gran to Meade House in Long Farnden.

NINE

꒰

"DID YOU SEE IT, DEREK?" LOIS SAID. SHE WAS SITTING with her feet up on the sofa, drinking a cup of tea and had just finished watching her favourite detective series.

"See what?" Derek had been sleeping off a good lunch, and now surfaced.

"The cat. Dead. Discovered under the floor at the Mill. Dried with age and hideously stretched out under a glass cover. It was found when they converted the mill to a hotel. They've got a label next to it, telling its history."

"Witchcraft," said Gran. "The old superstition that a dead cat, walled up alive sometimes, would keep evil spirits at bay. It would have been put there when the building was first erected. That mill is very old, you know. I think it's very creepy, and I always walk well away from it if I'm in reception.

They say the cat was moved in the recent renovations, and now would bring bad luck. Shouldn't have been moved, they say."

"A load of rubbish!" said Derek, fully awake now. "They should have given the thing a decent burial and forgotten about it. To change the subject, did you really enjoy your party, me duck? The kids did most of the organising. I was really proud of them."

"And we were certainly safe from gate-crashers with two policemen in the party," said Lois, smiling broadly.

"Very nice to see Matthew looking so handsome," said Gran. "Can't say the same for Cowgill."

Lois knew this was said to annoy her, and didn't answer.

NEXT MORNING, SOON AFTER BREAKFAST, THE PHONE RANG, AND Lois went to her office to answer it. It was Aurora Black, and she was in tears.

"Aurora! Are you okay? Take it slowly, and tell me what's up."

"It's Donald. He's sitting in a chair staring into space and refusing to answer. His Farnden jewellery party is tomorrow, and he wouldn't want me to cancel it. I don't know why I'm bothering you, but I didn't know who else to talk to."

"I'm glad you did. Now, when did this come on? Was he all right when you got up this morning? And did Milly manage a visit?"

"No. Last-minute emergency. I think that may have upset Donald. You know how he adores her! Yes. He is a bit quiet normally, but nothing like he is now. Should I ring the doctor?"

"Not unless you think he is in pain, or likely to do anything silly."

"Like committing suicide, do you mean? I hadn't even thought of that. He's usually such a jolly soul. Always makes the best of things, even when the business isn't doing too well."

"How is it doing now? Do you think he might be depressed? In the clinical sense, I mean. One of my cleaning girls had a patch of that. It's a real illness when it's bad."

There was a sort of scuffling noise at the other end of the phone line, and then a cry from Aurora. Donald's voice came on, nearly deafening Lois.

"If that's Lois Meade, you can mind your own business. Aurora has got herself in a bother for nothing. I shall be in Farnden as planned."

"But—" Lois began, but the call was cut off. She replaced the receiver and drew a deep breath. What on earth was all that about? She thought of ringing again to speak to Aurora, but decided not. It might make matters worse.

She looked at her schedules, due to be discussed at the meeting at lunchtime, and put them to one side. She had had a ringround telling all the cleaners that, if possible, they should come in as usual after all, as one or two things had come up. The meeting shouldn't take long, she had assured them, as they had already done the schedules and paperwork.

Who among her circle of friends and colleagues would be likely to know more about Donald Black?

Dot. Dot Nimmo, of course. She knew everybody, and might well have some useful background knowledge on

Aurora's husband. Why did he say she should mind her own business? What did he think she knew about him that was suspicious?

Too many questions now. If he had wanted to keep her out of something, he had not been very clever. She went back to her papers for the Brooms meeting. Dot would be sure to be coming along, and she would keep her back for a chat.

BEFORE THEY BEGAN, LOIS THANKED THE GIRLS AND ANDREW for the birthday card they had sent, and described her wonderful party.

"It's such a lovely setting, by the old millpond, with all the ducks and swans, and that huge weeping willow overhanging it. Have you been there, Dot?"

"Not since the mill has been turned into a hotel. O'course, when it was working full blast, everywhere around it was dusted with white flour. All the blokes who worked there. Even the bosses went white before their time! But we used to take our dog and walk on the water meadows. Midsummer, they used to have a regatta on the river. That was a lovely day. My Handy was a good rower, and he used to win prizes."

The others listened, and smiled. They all knew that Dot's husband, Handel, was a respectable crook. Nobody came to any harm from the Nimmo gang, but they amassed a good deal of illegally earned income over the years. Dot drove an expensive car, and bought designer clothes.

"Are any of you coming to the jewellery party this evening? It's at seven thirty in our village hall. Donald Black, from Brigham."

"Is that him whose wife runs a bakery opposite the hotel?"

Hazel had come in late from the Tresham office, but now sat comfortably enjoying Dot's reminiscences.

"That's the one," said Lois. "I shall be going, to support Aurora. And Gran said she'd come. Not to buy anything, of course! Too old for jewellery, she says. There'll be coffee and cake, so should be fun. It would be nice if some of you could come along, and don't forget New Brooms secret motto: 'Ears and eyes open.'"

"I'll be there," said Dot loyally. "Though I must say I prefer the real thing."

"Lucky old you, to be able to afford it," said Andrew. "I don't think it's quite the thing for chaps."

The meeting wound up, and the girls drifted away.

"Oh Dot! Can you spare a couple of minutes?" called Lois.

"Nothing wrong, I hope, Mrs. M?" said Dot.

"No, it's only that I wanted to pick your brains about Donald Black. I believe he's from a local family?"

"Ah," said Dot. "So that's it. I had a policeman round asking questions after that murder, but I told him I knew nothing."

"And is that true?"

"Sort of. I don't know much about Donald Black the chief executive of Brigham Jewellery, but plenty about Donald the likely lad with an eye for the ladies. I used to live next door to his Nan. That was his grandmother, and he called her Nan."

"So what was he like? I suppose he must be in his fifties now."

"Yeah. He was at school with me, but a bit of a duffer. Slow learner, I suppose you'd call him now. In them days, the slow ones got left out. Left to fend for themselves after they finished school. He was always good looking though, with his black hair and nice smiley face. He did a few jobs for my Handy's organisation."

"What sort of jobs?" said Lois.

"Oh, this and that. Sometimes valuable stuff, like jewellery an' similar, used to pass through Nimmo hands, and he always liked being involved with that. I reckon that's why he set up his own business, but with sparkly tat. He does pretty well now, so I've been told."

"Still involved with your Nimmo lot?"

"Not *my* lot anymore, Mrs. M. I'd rather work for you. But I do still see one or two of them. I could ask around, if you like."

Lois knew she need not explain any more to Dot. She would know that it was a ferretin' matter, and something useful might come up.

TEN

"WE'RE HAVING EARLY SUPPER," SAID GRAN. "ME AND Lois are going to the village hall to buy ourselves some of the crown jewels. Stolen goods, you know."

Derek laughed. "Not what I heard," he said. "That Donald Black has quite a way with the women, so I'm told. You'd better be prepared to resist being offered more than you bargained for."

"Are you serious?" said Lois. "The poor man is only trying to earn a living. He goes all round the country with his parties. Aurora says he's exhausted when he comes back."

"Very likely a girl in every port," said Gran. "Could be very exhausting."

Lois was about to say that Donald and Aurora seemed to have a very happy marriage, but then remembered the telephone call. He had sounded angry, and Aurora scared.

"Well, we're not being invited on to the board of his business, so I expect we'll be all right," she said.

THE VILLAGE HALL WAS CROWDED BY THE TIME GRAN AND LOIS had collected Josie and made their way inside. They found chairs and sat down, acknowledging friends and contributing to the din of conversation.

"Good evening, ladies," said Donald. He sat at a long table, where he and Aurora had spread out the jewellery to show it at its best. "And one gentleman, I see. Welcome, sir."

He then gave a preliminary spiel, and suggested that they came out in fours to allow room for people to choose.

"And then," he continued, "we'll break for coffee and have a little time for you to have another browse, in case you've remembered an auntie with a birthday coming up!"

Then he introduced a good-looking redheaded model, who tried items on her creamy skin to show customers exactly how necklaces and earrings would look. The scheme worked well. Aurora helped out, wrapping purchases and advising doubters. When all customers had had a chance to buy, Donald called for a coffee break. He and Aurora, and the model, whose name was Gloria, moved among the crowd as they were served, and chatted in a friendly way. They handed out advertising leaflets, and were well received.

"They don't push you to buy," said Gran approvingly. "I'll read this when I get home. Where's the lone man that Donald Black welcomed? I should think he came in out of the rain and scarpered when he saw what he'd blundered into!"

"It's not raining," said Lois. "He's still around somewhere.

I reckon he is some kind of stooge, meant to infiltrate the crowd and encourage them."

"Trust you to be suspicious!" said Gran. "Come on, Josie. Let's go and have another look before we leave."

They walked off, leaving Lois to her coffee, and in a few seconds, Aurora came and sat beside her.

"Are you enjoying yourself?" she said. "It's a good crowd, and Donald is pleased."

"Who's the single bloke? I see he's still here. Is he with one of the women?"

Aurora looked embarrassed. "No, he's one of the business employees. Peter Fountain. Same family as Sylvia. A sort of security guard. We do get shoplifters sometimes. It's quite easy for a skilled operator to slide a piece of jewellery into a waiting handbag!"

"Has it happened this evening?"

"Don't know yet. I don't think so. Would you like some more coffee?"

"No thanks. We must be off soon. Gran has spotted a butterfly brooch and Josie fancies a bracelet, so when all that's done, we'll be on our way. An enjoyable evening, anyway, Aurora, and Donald seems quite better from his funny turn."

Aurora nodded. "Thanks for coming. Have you got a leaflet? You might like to have a go at what he suggests. Some of the women seem to be filling in the forms. See you later, Lois."

BACK HOME IN MEADE HOUSE, GRAN SHOWED DEREK HER brooch, and it was duly admired.

"There's this leaflet, Derek. You have a read of it and tell us what it says." The print was quite small, and Gran was reluctant to admit that she needed new glasses.

Derek took the leaflet and read it in silence. Then he frowned. "I reckon it's one of them pyramid selling jobs," he said. "This asks if you want to be a seller, like the Black bloke. You get lots of advice and help, and all you need to do is become a member, which means paying a membership fee, and buying a collection of jewellery and have parties, like him. And here's the catch. They want you to enroll a couple of friends or interested customers into the scheme themselves."

"Oh Lord," said Lois. "I don't like the sound of that. I thought those kind of schemes were illegal. The man at the top gets off scot-free, with a sizeable loot, and by the time you get to the bottom of the pyramid, you can be deeply in debt. We shall have nothing to do with it, Mum."

Gran did not like being told what to do, and so said she would give it some careful thought. She quite fancied the idea, she said. "I'd be good at selling," she said. "Remember Woolworths, Lois? You and me had our regular customers and did really well. You on confectionary and me on jewellery. I had the brains and you the beauty!"

"Oh, for heaven's sake, Mother! There's a lot of difference between weighing out a quarter of aniseed balls and dealing in expensive jewellery."

"Quite right," said Derek. "And it's not the jewellery that's at the heart of it, though you'd have to buy it from Donald Black. It's deceiving people into committing themselves to a scheme that gets to be impossible in the end, and you'd end up in debt."

Gran was not convinced. She took back the leaflet. "Well, it looks good to me. There's pictures here of women who've made a small fortune for themselves and enjoyed it in the process. Look, Lois."

"I've looked. Give it to me, and I'll put it in the bin."

Gran was having none of it, and retired to her bedroom, taking the leaflet with her.

ELEVEN

❧

Next morning, as soon as Lois sat down in her office chair, the phone rang.

"Mrs. M? It's Dot here. Did you go to that jewellery knees-up last night?"

"Yes, we did. Bought one or two things. They were really nice. Didn't see you there."

"I went late. They were starting to pack up, but were very nice and helpful. Your friend Aurora is especially pleasant. I reckon he'd be lost without her. Anyway, when I'd bought a pair of earrings, they gave me this leaflet. Did you get one? I must say I'm tempted to have a go. Once you've paid your membership fee, it looks foolproof. I haven't seen one of these things since I bought that plastic kitchen stuff that was all the go. What did you think?"

"I think I've got enough to do, what with New Brooms

and the family. Jamie's home for four weeks, and we want to see as much as possible of him. We're going to a recital he's giving in Birmingham next week."

"I notice you don't mention ferretin'. That's why I've called you."

Lois's voice changed. "Have you got something on Donald Black? You've hardly had time to talk to your Nimmos."

"Can I come and see you? I'm not happy about the phone. You never know when somebody's listening in."

"Dot! The days are long past when the telephonist on the local switchboard put down her knitting to listen to calls! But yes, come over this afternoon. About three?"

Dot agreed and ended the call. Lois picked up a letter of complaint that had come in from a man who said Floss had stolen all his savings when she was dusting his bedroom. She sighed. She had considered ending New Brooms contract with this customer. Every week he had a complaint. He was elderly and living alone, and she felt sorry for him. But accusing a cleaner of stealing money was not on, and she made a note to call in on him later. She knew that by the time she went, he would have forgotten all about it and deny it hotly. But still, the poor old sod was lonely, so she decided to tell Floss to ignore it and carry on as usual.

She put the letter down and sat back in her chair. The jewellery party had obviously been a success, and the model had talked interestingly about her training for the catwalk. But how many more women had been tempted by the seller scheme? She thought of Aurora, a quiet, sensible and, she was sure, completely trustworthy friend. But she was also the wife of Donald Black, who was always jolly and charming . . . Or was he? What was that last phone call all about? He had sounded bullying and unpleasant. And Aurora was frightened. Maybe they had had a row about Milly not coming home? Possible.

Lois sighed again. Did all this mean she had to have a serious conversation with Aurora, or should she mind her own business and let them get on with it? Never come between man and wife, Gran said often, and she was right, nine times out of ten. Was this the tenth? She shook her head. Dot was coming this afternoon, and perhaps she would have the answer.

Lois stood up and went to the window to look down the street. Not much happening. A small group of children from the school was out on a nature ramble. A car drew up outside, and she watched the door open. It was Douglas, and then Jamie got out of the passenger side. He saw her at the window and waved. She cheered up at once. Her boys! It was so seldom they were together, and still getting on well.

Jamie had become friendly with a girl reporter on the local newspaper, and their friendship had survived, although interrupted by one or two other girls and in spite of his constant travelling and her reluctance to give up her job and follow him. Derek had had a quiet word with his son and told him to get moving and hitch the girl up before someone else got there before him. Lois was amused, and wondered if Jamie had come home to pop the question.

Lunch was a lively occasion, with Gran and her grandsons and Derek and Lois enjoying it all. After they'd finished and were sitting watching a match on the telly, Lois asked Douglas if he could spare a minute in her office.

"What's up, Mum?" he said, as she closed the office door. "All this hush-hush stuff?"

"So," SAID GRAN, WHEN HE EMERGED. "WHAT HAS OUR OWN private investigator wanted from you, Douglas?"

"A bit embarrassing, Gran. What used to be called 'flies undone' and me a chief executive of an important company! Good old Mum. Bless her. Whoever invented zips should be throttled."

Twelve

༈

A FTER Douglas and Jamie had gone, Lois said Dot would be coming for a quick talk at three, and after that she would be going over to Brigham to collect the bread. Would Gran like to come for a drive? Gran accepted with alacrity. She did not get many such invitations from Lois, but accepted that most of Lois's expeditions were to do with New Brooms, or ferretin'.

"I'll change me shoes, and then I'll be ready," she said. "It'll be nice to see your friend Aurora again. She was a great help at the jewellery party."

"One thing, Mother," Lois said. "No mention of you being interested in becoming a seller. Steer well clear of that one."

Gran agreed meekly. She omitted to mention that she had the leaflet safe in her pocket.

*   *   *

DOT ARRIVED PROMPTLY AT THREE O'CLOCK, AND JOINED LOIS IN her study. She was unsmiling and not her usual bouncy self.

"What's up, then, Dot?" said Lois.

"It's that Donald Black. You know you asked me to see if my shady relations knew anything about him? Well, they did. Mostly because the chiropodist that he worked for a while is none other than my cousin-in-law, Elgar Windrush. Lovely name, ain't it, Mrs. M?"

Lois nodded, not sure where this was leading.

"Well, Mister Sparkly Black was discovered with his hand in the till. Not as such, but he did the books for my cousin, and when the tax man requested an interview, they discovered Donald had adjusted the profits, siphoning off some for himself."

"Goodness! So what happened. I've never heard a whiff of scandal from Aurora."

Dot raised her eyebrows. "Well, you wouldn't, would you. It was all hushed up. He paid a whopping fine, and no more was said. Except that he got the push from the chiropodist. Natch."

Lois thanked Dot, passed on a compliment from a satisfied housewife who had found Dot extremely satisfactory, and waved her off to her next client.

WHEN LOIS AND GRAN ARRIVED OUTSIDE THE BAKERY, LOIS repeated the warning to her smiling mother. Aurora saw them coming, and was at the door to welcome them. "Hi, Lois! Lovely to see you, Mrs. Weedon," she said. "Come on in. Most of my customers have been today, so why don't I put on the kettle and we'll have a cuppa and one of these muffins, fresh from the oven."

"Very nice," said Gran, beaming. "That's a very kind thought, Mrs. Black."

"Oh, do call me Aurora, please."

Off to a good start, thought Lois. "I can take over if you have to see to a customer," she said.

Gran immediately tackled the subject of selling jewellery, exactly as Lois had expected. "How long has your husband been in the jewellery business?" Gran asked, balancing a plate with muffin on her lap. "He certainly seems to know all about it."

"Oh, well, about three years, I suppose. He was in chiropody before that."

"Got fed up with handling people's feet, I expect," Gran said knowledgeably.

Aurora laughed. "He didn't actually do the treatments, Mrs. Weedon. He was more on the bookkeeping side. He's not properly qualified to practise, though he'd sometimes help out if his boss was overworked. He massages my feet sometimes, and it is really relaxing."

"That's what you need, Lois," said Gran. "When you've been running around all day. Does he take private patients? Go on, Lois, I'll treat you."

Lois said she'd think about it, but could they talk about something else? Smelly feet were putting her off her muffin. Aurora agreed, and said she would ask Donald but expected him to refuse, as he was not qualified.

"Right, Lois," said Gran. "Am I allowed to ask about the parties and the sellers, and how the whole thing works? Without personally committing myself, of course. I am only curious, Aurora, as everybody had such a great time."

"And the customers are also the winners, of course," said Aurora.

"How d'you mean?" asked Gran.

"Well, people who buy are encouraged to become members and hold a party themselves. It is all legal and aboveboard."

"And is part of the deal that they then have to get friends to hold parties in their turn?" Lois kept her voice light.

At that moment, the door opened, and Donald walked in. He made a little bow to Gran and took her hand. "Delighted to meet you, Mrs. Weedon," he said. "And Lois, how are you keeping? I owe you a little apology for my bad temper on the phone. I had a really severe headache, but that's no excuse. Is there another cup in the pot, Aurora?"

He sat down next to Gran, and asked if she had enjoyed the party. She was about to answer when the shop doorbell rang.

Aurora was pouring tea, and asked Lois if she would mind holding on to the customer until she had finished. "Donald likes it exactly right," she said.

Lois walked through to the shop, where she found Inspector Cowgill eyeing the cakes.

"Cowgill! Are you following me about?"

"Of course I'm not," he said. "I always collect my bread

from Mrs. Black on a Tuesday. Is she around, or are you adding shopkeeper to your many skills?"

"She's coming in a second. I've brought Mum over, for a little drive out."

"And you just happened to end up in Brigham? Don't worry, Lois, my dear. I won't tread on your toes. That's my wholemeal loaf, over there on the shelf. Always the same place. And here's the money. Good luck, my dear. I'll be in touch."

He took his bread and was out of the shop in seconds, before Aurora came in to take over.

"Oh yes," she said. "Inspector Cowgill always comes in about this time. Nice man, isn't he? His wife died, you know. But it was a long time ago. He should find another nice woman to take care of him. Sometimes he looks very sad."

"Mm, well, it's a funny old job, isn't it?" said Lois. "The police are always seeing the wrong side of mankind. It can't be much fun. Anyway, thanks for the tea and being nice to Mum. You won't let her do anything silly, will you, Aurora? She seemed to be much too involved with the subject when talking to Donald."

When they went back to join Gran and Donald, they found them still deep in conversation about percentages and investments.

"Your mother, Lois, has a very good business head on her shoulders. I expect it is where you get yours from!" Donald helped Gran to her feet, though she did not need it, and escorted them to the car.

"See you soon, both of you, I hope," he said. "My daughter is coming from London to see us soon, so we must meet," he said, and stood with Aurora to wave them goodbye.

*   *   *

DEREK WAS STILL OUT AT WORK WHEN THEY REACHED HOME, and Gran set about preparing supper. "Fishcakes and beans tonight," she said. "And fruit for pudding. I'm off to whist with Joan. In the village hall. Why don't you come, Lois?"

"Because I hate whist," said Lois. "As I have said many times. You go and enjoy yourself, Mother dear. I shall have a nice time watching telly with my husband. Just we two. We might even have a cup of hot chocolate with cream in it. Ah, there's Derek. You can tell him about your heart-to-heart with Donald Black."

"What's that about Donald Black?" said Derek, coming into the kitchen. "Not my favourite person, as you know. I hope you haven't invited him to supper, Elsie!"

"And if I have?" said Gran defensively. "I'm allowed to have my own friends, aren't I?"

Neither Lois nor Derek answered, and Lois departed with Jeems into the garden, while Derek fled upstairs to wash his hands.

Thirteen

༠

WEDNESDAY WAS MARKET DAY IN TRESHAM, AND LOIS went in every week to shop from the local stalls, including butchers, fishmongers (fresh fish, though they couldn't be farther from the sea), and homegrown vegetables. There were also several stalls selling home-baked goodies, and the fragrance of homegrown herbs alone made them impossible to resist.

If she arrived home with her bags full, she knew Derek and Gran would both be offended. He had a productive vegetable garden, and Gran prided herself on her baking. "I like to have a change, that's all," she usually protested. Today, she bought only veg and fruit not grown by Derek, and coconut biscuits not made by Gran.

"Anything for a peaceful life," she muttered, and then turned round swiftly as she felt a hand on her shoulder.

"Morning, Mrs. Meade," said Cowgill, smiling sweetly at her.

"Don't *do* that!" she said. "Heavy hand of the law, an' all that. Are you shopping too?"

"Sort of."

"Well, don't let me keep you."

"I've done it all, anyway. Fancy a coffee?"

Lois hesitated. Cowgill might have some further information on Donald Black.

"Okay, then. But it'll have to be a quick one. Gran puts lunch on the table at one o'clock precisely, whether there's anyone there to eat it or not."

Lois chose a table in the corner of the café, and sat with her back to the door. Well trained by Cowgill, she did not want to obstruct his view of the marketplace. His eyes flicked from corner to corner while they had coffee, and he seemed distracted when Lois asked him about Donald Black.

"Oh, he's a charlatan, Lois. Nothing serious, as far as we know, but we keep an eye on his jewellery parties. Those things can end up bankrupting perfectly innocent people."

"Such as Gran?"

He snapped instantly to attention. "Gran, did you say? Good heavens, I hope she hasn't been taken in by his pretty ways!"

"She's pretending not to have been, but I know my mum. She gets an idea into her head, and won't let it rest until she's cracked it."

"Just like someone else I know. But you must not let her get involved, Lois. She is exactly the sort of intelligent person who thinks she can back out whenever she chooses, and then finds that she can't."

"It's all very well to say that. You should try changing my mum's mind when she's decided on something. And she's very touchy about the family interfering with her savings. Says she's earned every penny and intends to spend it her way."

Cowgill could see that his Lois was really worried, and reached across the small table to take her hand. Lois immediately withdrew it, and said what would people think if they saw them sitting hand in hand in a public place?

His laughter caused heads to turn, and he shook his head. "My dear Lois," he said, "what can I say? I will certainly keep an eye on Black for you, but if I were you I would enlist the help of Aurora. She works closely with him running the bakery, and can sound the alarm if Gran is getting in too deep."

"What do you know about his past?"

"Only that he had a job with the local chiropodist, who terminated his contract after trouble with the tax inspector. Nothing came of it, and then he began publicising his jewellery parties. He knows the law, and skates pretty close to it, but so far, so good. If you do find any connection between him and the Fountain case, I'd be glad to hear from you."

Lois drained her coffee cup and said that she must be on her way. "Good hunting, Cowgill. Nothing but good news from my daughter and your nephew. Josie seems in good spirits, and the two of them are off on holiday next week. I must say they are welcome to the crowds. It's school holidays, and Marbella would not be my choice."

He rose to his feet, but after she had gone, he ordered

another coffee and sat down to think. It was certainly surprising that Gran Weedon had been so taken in by the golden-voiced Black. He would have said she was proof against any erosion of her savings. Perhaps she was genuinely interested in knowing how the scheme worked, and would see off Black in her characteristically forthright way.

FOURTEEN

✥

"I'M GLAD TO SEE YOU HAVEN'T WASTED OUR HOUSEKEEPING money on fripperies, anyway," said Gran, after she had examined Lois's purchases.

They had decided long ago that they would have a joint housekeeping account, where each would make a one-third contribution each week. It worked reasonably well, and Lois kept a separate wallet with her own money in case she spotted something Gran would disapprove of.

Sometimes, Lois would feel like a child at the mercies of her mother's wrath. But most of the time she maintained a tactful silence to keep the peace. Now she felt virtuous, and on reflection realised how ridiculous the whole thing had become. Still, as they sat down to lunch, Gran's mind was on other things.

"What are we doing this coming weekend?" she asked.

"It's the County Agricultural Show in Waltonby, and Joan and I thought we might go. We can catch a bus at two, and another to come home around five. It'll give us time to look around the stalls, and see what's going on in the show rings. Joan loves the horses, and I favour the cattle. Especially the great bulls! You wouldn't happen to be going, either of you? Then we could have a lift."

"Don't think so, Gran," said Derek. "I shall have to work on Saturday to get a job finished. How about you, Lois? You three could be girls together?" Joan was Gran's best friend and lived just around the corner from Meade House. Lois approved this friendship warmly, as Joan was brilliant at keeping Gran from some of her more serious excesses for brightening their lives. The show might take Gran's mind off jewellery, with any luck.

"Thanks and no thanks! I really don't know, Mum, but if I do go, I'll certainly give you and Joan a lift."

Lois was immediately suspicious. Gran usually steered clear of the big shows, saying her old feet were too tired to be tramping round fields.

"Has Josie got any programmes of events and exhibitors in the shop? She does sometimes sell them in advance, so you don't have to wait in a queue at the gate. I'll pop down this afternoon and see. Anything you want, Mum?"

"I should have thought you'd done enough shopping for one day! Still, if you're going, we could do with more milk."

THE SHOP WAS BUSY WHEN LOIS ARRIVED, MOSTLY DUE TO A gaggle of women who had the local paper in their hands.

Lois could see the front page with a banner headline, POLICE BAFFLED BY FOUNTAIN CASE.

"The cops don't have far to look!" said one.

At this point, Josie said in the nicest possible way that if the ladies had no more shopping to do, perhaps they could carry on talking outside. Looking huffy, they reluctantly stepped outside the shop and dispersed.

"Hi, Mum, I've kept the local for you. As you saw, it's a popular newspaper today! Have you come to shop or chat?"

"Both," said Lois. "Milk for Gran, and I was wondering if you have any programmes for the County Agricultural Show on Saturday?"

Like a conjurer, Josie delved behind a pile of chocolate bars and came up with a handful of programmes.

"Compliments of the shop," she said, handing one to Lois.

"No, for heaven's sake, Josie. It's ten pounds to go in if you pay at the gate."

"Only five pounds at this shop," Josie said.

"How much of that goes to you, then?"

"Half. Two pounds fifty. The charge at the gate includes parking round the rings. Anyway, why so interested in the show?"

Lois put a five pound note on the counter, and took a programme.

"It's a good day out, usually. Are you going? Is Matthew on duty there?"

Josie shook her head. "I'm here until four. Matthew may go, but off duty."

*   *   *

BACK HOME, LOIS WENT STRAIGHT TO HER OFFICE AND OPENED the programme. She flipped through lists of agricultural-machinery manufacturers and clothing for the countryman and -woman, and came to a section for the craft marquee. Albrights Liquor Store, followed by Brigham Bakery—that would be Aurora—and then, yes, there it was, "Brighten Up for Summer with Brigham Luxury Jewellery."

So, was this the reason Mum was so keen to go?

Lois had planned to work all day in her office, updating her accounts, but now decided the best way to find out would be to offer Joan and Mum a lift, and then keep an eye on them.

FIFTEEN

 ❧

THE REST OF THE WEEK, LOIS HAD SPENT WORKING ON HER accounts, until she threw up her hands in despair and put all her invoices and receipts in an old attaché case and dumped it on a friendly Tresham accountant's desk.

Derek said he didn't know why she didn't save herself all that frustration and time, and take it to him in the first place. She replied that she used to be good at maths at school, but that was not apparently enough. Every year the whole horrible subject of tax returns became more complicated.

Derek replied that her consequent bad temper lasted at least a couple of weeks, and he offered to pay the accountant's fees if that would solve the problem.

Now it was Saturday, and the County Agricultural Show day. The village had been woken by a head-to-tail queue of moving cars, horse boxes and vast trailers carrying machinery as high as the bedroom windows.

"Shall we go up this morning instead of afternoon?" Lois said. "I would say most of the interesting things happen in the morning."

Gran shook her head. "No, Lois. Joan has to go to the hairdresser's this morning. We'll go at two as planned."

Lois's suspicions were growing. When they drove into the show ground, and parked some way from the rings, Gran said she and Joan would go off by themselves, as she didn't want an argument with Lois about what they should look at. They would meet in the refreshment tent at four. Would that suit?

There was no reason to disagree, so Lois loitered round the first few stalls, until she could no longer be seen by Gran, then began to follow at a distance. She looked at the map of the show ground, and saw that the craft marquee was directly opposite the entrance gate. Taking her time, she sauntered past grain traders and the National Farmers Union tent, where members were quaffing free drinks. It was hot and crowded, visitors making the most of the spring weather, and the ice cream van was doing good business. Small girls and their mothers kitted out for pony classes picnicked on the grass by their horse boxes.

A former client called out to Lois to join them on their seats at the ringside. "Haven't seen you for *ages,* Mrs. Meade!"

Lois shouted thanks, but sauntered on. She approached the craft marquee cautiously, deliberately turning her face away as she entered. Standing behind a crowd at the home-brewing stall, she glanced quickly around. Her heart lurched, as she saw the big sign advertising Brigham Luxury Jewellery. Busy talking from behind the display was Gran, her face flushed and excited. Behind her, Joan was wrapping up a purchase. Neither of them saw her, and she slipped away, walking rapidly to sit on a straw bale at the ringside to consider what she should do next.

Sixteen

❧

"DID YOU HAVE A GOOD TIME, GIRLS?" SAID DEREK, AS they sat down to a sandwich supper. "There's still show traffic going through the village. The trailers and horse boxes hold them up, going slowly. You'd think they'd reroute them."

"I reckon it was the biggest show so far," said Gran. "Me and Joan won a bottle of wine on the lottery, and lost money on the lucky dip. I thought the craft marquee was rubbish this year. What did you think, Lois? We didn't see you."

"I missed it," she lied. "Spent most of my time talking to old friends and clients. It's a great day for meeting people. I loved the parade, and the foxhounds with the master. It was a shame one of the hounds turned nasty with a young boy, but no great harm done, apparently. Dogs are dogs, and even Jeems can turn savage with black Labradors."

Gran looked relieved. She had been prepared to brazen it out if Lois had come into the marquee, but now she knew she could relax. She had thought she caught sight of the back of her head, but it obviously wasn't Lois. It had been so exciting, and she had taken a respectable amount of money for Donald. He had confirmed that her own supply of jewellery would be arriving soon. She and Joan had agreed to sign up as members on a trial basis, with an opt-out clause if they decided against it. If they went ahead, they would each recruit a couple of friends from other villages. It was so easy! She had decided not to tell Lois and Derek until their jewellery arrived, when it would be too late for a fuss. Donald suggested that as he had so recently had a party in the village, they should perhaps go farther afield. He would be on hand to help throughout.

"So what else did you and Joan see, Mum?"

Gran shrugged. "Oh, all the usual things. I saw some very pretty little bantams, and nearly bought a couple for you."

"I'm pretty well up to capacity, thanks, Mum. Did you see the bulls, your favourites? I saw that beautiful Hereford got first prize again."

Gran nodded. "He certainly deserved it," she said, without actually admitting to not having seen it.

Lois had hoped to catch her out, knowing that the red rosette had gone to a glamorous-looking creamy beast, nothing like the Hereford. But Gran was a match for her. She knew exactly how to avoid committing herself, and Lois gave up.

Derek, however, asked a number of questions, wanting to know if his many farmer friends had been there and if Gran had chatted to any of them. It became obvious that she hadn't seen a single one, and Lois's suspicion that she and Joan had spent the whole time on the jewellery stall was confirmed.

Later on, when Gran had retired to her own room, obviously quite exhausted by her afternoon's adventure, Lois told Derek what she had seen, and to her surprise, he said he knew already. One of his friends had stopped his car on the way home from the show, and said he had seen his mother-in-law in the craft tent.

"What did you say to him?" said Lois.

"Not much. I asked if he was sure, and he said there was only one Mrs. Weedon, and he knew Joan, too. Shall we have to find out what they are up to, before it goes any further?"

"It'd be better to wait until Gran tells us herself, and then we can always get her out of trouble, if necessary. She looked like she'd had a new lease on life, chatting to customers at the stall. And, by the way, I saw something else a bit odd."

"Don't keep me in suspense," said Derek.

"There was a huge refreshment tent, and in one corner, behind a great palm tree in a pot, I saw Donald himself, cosying up to a redhead who looked as if she wouldn't be seen dead at an agricultural show, wouldn't know one end of a cow from the other. She was familiar, and might have been the model who was at the jewellery party, but I couldn't see her very well."

"Where was Aurora? Wasn't she at the show?"

"I don't think so," said Lois. "The bakery is open until half past five as usual. Oh dear, that Donald Black is even more of a fool than I thought. Obviously, we say nothing."

"What do we say nothing about?" said Gran, appearing at the door with her hair in a hairnet and her face shining with moisturising cream. "Have you seen my book? Barbara Taylor Bradford's best. I want to read it again."

Lois found the book and wished her mother a good night's sleep. "You'll know how it ends, won't you?"

"Perhaps this time she goes off with the rogue and lives happily ever after?" said Derek.

"And goodnight to you two, too!" said Gran crossly, and disappeared.

The truth was that she was sure she would not be able to get to sleep, her mind whizzing round the afternoon's events. She settled back into bed and opened her book. Five minutes later, she was fast asleep and snoring contentedly.

"We're nearly out of bread," said Gran, as Lois and Derek appeared for breakfast. "We had a bit of a run on it for sandwiches yesterday. We could get a loaf from Josie. She's open until twelve. I shall be going to the morning service with Joan. It's a shortened matins, so I could go straight down after, if you like?"

"I thought of going over to Brigham this morning," said Lois. "I need to chat to Aurora about a New Brooms client, so I can get bread at the same time. Her shop opens for a couple of hours, and I'm sure she will have a spare loaf for me. Lunch at the usual time?"

"One o'clock prompt." Gran was uneasy. Would Lois be going to pump Aurora about the jewellery? She had asked

Donald if they could both keep quiet until she was ready to tell the family herself. She knew Lois and Aurora were good friends.

SIX MILES AWAY, IN THE WARM KITCHEN OF THE BAKERY, AURORA was listening to an account from Donald of yesterday's show. He seemed very pleased at the result of the day's takings.

"Our stall," he said, "was the only decent one in the craft marquee. And Elsie Weedon and her friend Joan were amazing! I had chosen fairly unglitzy stuff, guessing they would attract the older women, and they shifted a very respectable lot. Of course, they knew a lot of the farmers' wives and so on. I should think they are in for a good career! And they won't want to do it forever, so we won't have any difficulties, with luck."

"I'm not so happy about it, as you know, Donald. Lois Meade is a good friend of mine, and I wouldn't want to cause her any worries. They must be in their early seventies at least. And you know as well as I do that there is a lot of work in organising a jewellery party."

"But I shall be there, helping them all the way, and once into the swing of it, I am sure they'll be fine. After all, they can recruit younger people to help."

After that, they did not talk for an hour or so. Aurora was busy in the bakery, and Donald disappeared into his office to work. When the phone rang, Donald picked up the house phone.

"Good morning! Can I help you?"

"Ah, Lois here, Donald. Is it okay if I pop over this

morning for a couple of loaves? We seem to have run out earlier than usual. But do say if it's not convenient."

"It'll be fine, Lois. Never turn away customers; that's my motto. How's your mother this morning? Oops, I forgot! You're not supposed to know. But anyway, she and Joan did a brilliant job yesterday. They offered to help, and in no time at all, they had taken over, and I left them to it."

And I hope that's all there was to it, thought Lois. She feared this was not so, but said she would be there in half an hour, and looked forward to hearing more about the show. She supposed she had better not mention the redhead.

Seventeen

ॐ

Brigham was a pretty village, and the Mill House Hotel looked good enough to star in a movie, with the pond in dappled sunlight from the overhanging willow. On an impulse, after Aurora closed up the bakery, Lois decided to take her over for a drink in the hotel bar, where the big windows looked across water meadows. Perhaps they would take Jeems for a walk first, instead of shutting her up in the car.

Aurora was delighted with the suggestion, and, leaving Donald to look after himself, they set off cheerfully, with Jeems straining at the lead.

After a gentle stroll to the river and round by the rushing weir, they came back to the hotel and decided on a cold cider to cool themselves.

"But first the toilet!" said Aurora, heading for the hotel

ladies' room. Lois fetched Jemima's bowl of water from the back of the van, which she moved into the shade. With Jeems safely on the lead attached to the car, she went back to find a table by the window looking over the meadows.

Finally settled with chilled cider, Aurora said how much she had enjoyed their walk. She lived so near the hotel, but seldom went in for any reason other than to sell bread and supplies for the restaurant.

"Lois, forgive me if I'm wrong," she continued, "but did you have another reason to come over today? I know your Josie sells bread, and opens up for the papers on Sundays."

"Her bread is not a patch on yours, I'm afraid," said Lois.

"No other reason?"

"Perhaps a batch of scones?"

"Don't avoid the question!" said Aurora, laughing. "I meant some other reason for coming over?"

"Well, I did wonder if my mother had signed up for anything with Donald. You know they manned the stall for him at the show?"

Aurora nodded. "Did you see them?"

"Yes, but they didn't see me."

"I think they decided on the spur of the moment to help him out. He had business with a client, he said, so it was a great help. I suppose you didn't see him?"

Warning lights came up in Lois's head, and she said no, she didn't think so.

"I think the client was young and blonde," said Aurora, her voice in a whisper.

"Ah, well that's another thing," said Lois. "I am sure you have nothing to worry about. Shall we have another?"

They sat for some time, chatting about this and that, and neither mentioned Gran and Joan again. They watched the big waterwheel turning slowly round and round, wet and dripping, its buckets spilling out as it moved.

In a pause in the conversation, Lois said that if Aurora didn't take her eyes off the wheel, she'd never focus properly again. Aurora laughed and was about to turn away, when her eye was caught by something on the wheel. Then she gasped and screamed, yelling, "Stop it! Stop the wheel!"

Slowly appearing from one side was a shoe, and as more people clustered round, shouting, "Stop the bloody wheel, can't you?" the soaking-wet body of a man in a suit and tie appeared spread-eagled across the top of the wheel.

Complete silence fell, and the wheel turned remorselessly on, spitting out its alien burden as it disappeared from sight.

Aurora crumpled to the floor, her hands covering her eyes, and Lois bent to help her. "It was him, wasn't it, Lois?" she whispered. "It was Donald?"

Lois could think of nothing to say, except, "Yes, it was."

Eighteen

❧

T HE LOVELY SUNNY MORNING AT BRIGHAM HAD TURNED into a horrific nightmare, and when Lois finally reached home, she had brought Aurora with her.

"I couldn't leave her by herself," she had said softly to Derek and Gran. "She has completely collapsed."

"No wonder!" said Gran. "Stretched out on the water-wheel, did you say? For goodness sake, how did he get there? You'd been at the bakery talking to the two of them not more than an hour previously?"

"More like a couple of hours," Lois said. "We went for a walk before going into the hotel for a drink. Anyway, she's asleep now, I think. I gave her one of my pills. The police will come knocking soon. I rang Matthew as soon as I could."

"And Cowgill?" said Derek.

"Of course," said Lois crossly. "He'll be coming over this

morning to talk to Aurora. I said we'd let him know when she was up and ready to talk. Are you all right, Mum? You're looking a bit seedy."

"Naturally! He had become a good friend in a short time. I don't know what Joan and I will do now."

"If you mean the jewellery parties, the whole thing will have to be put on hold until Aurora is able to take over. I think she knows all the details, and wouldn't want people to be left in the lurch."

"Just as well you and Joan hadn't got yourselves in too deep," said Derek, and immediately knew he was in trouble as Gran burst into tears.

"You have no cause to say such things!" she shouted at him through her sobs. "He was straight as a die, poor man."

"Quite right," said a weak voice from the doorway. Aurora stood there, still in a borrowed nightie, rubbing her eyes.

"I didn't dream it, did I?"

Lois went to her and put her arm around her shoulders. "No, I'm afraid not. But there's no need for you to worry about anything else at the moment. Inspector Cowgill is coming over to talk to you soon, but not until I give him the okay. Would you like some breakfast? Coffee or tea?"

Aurora shook her head. "Not at the moment, thanks Lois. Perhaps I'll have a shower and get dressed, and then I'll manage a cup of tea, if that's all right with you, Mrs. Weedon?"

"Of course, my dear. Why don't you call me Gran? Everyone else does, and it simplifies things."

After Aurora had gone upstairs, Lois turned on Derek. "That was the most tactless thing I can think of!" she said.

"Poor Aurora and then Gran. Isn't it time you were off to work? I thought you had to go early this week?"

"Odd as it might seem to you, Lois, I have stayed at home until I was sure the women in my care were all fit to be left, and to offer my help if needed."

Lois subsided. She crossed the kitchen, and Derek put his arms around her. "Buck up, me duck," he said, and kissed her gently. "I'm off now, but I'll be back at lunchtime. The job is over at Fletching, so it won't take me long."

Now Gran and Lois were left in the kitchen, and both sat down and stared at the table in silence. Then Gran said in her usual strong voice, "I don't know, I'm sure."

"Neither do I," said Lois. "But I intend to find out. Will you help, Mum? I wouldn't ask, but you did see quite a bit of him very recently."

"Of course I will. And I'm sure Joan will, too. We'll have to own up, won't we? We had agreed to be jewellery sellers, and had got as far as planning our first party in Fletching. Donald was going to help us all the way, he said."

"Had you handed over any cash?" Lois stared at her mother, sure that she would be able to detect a lying answer. "Honest?"

"Well, we had paid our membership fee, but there's a get-out clause. Honest, Lois."

"Thank God for that. At least we shan't have to fight to get it back."

"He said several times that his scheme was all aboveboard, and there was no catch to it. He were a good husband, Lois. Aurora will vouch for that."

Lois nodded, but she vividly remembered the angry telephone call and the redhead hiding behind a potted palm, not to mention rumours of Donald Black consorting with Sylvia Fountain in full view of his poor wife.

"At least Aurora has a watertight alibi," Gran continued, unaware of the aptness of the adjective. "She was with you from the time you said goodbye to him at the bakery to when you saw him on the wheel. Oh God, Lois! What a horrible way to die! How did he manage to get onto the wheel?"

"I expect the police will be looking at the wheel. The best we can hope for is that he was drowned in the deep water before the wheel got him."

"We don't know exactly how he died, do we?"

"Not yet. We'll probably know more when Cowgill gets here. I think I'll ring him now, and tell him to turn up in about an hour's time. In a way, the sooner Aurora can get through it, the better."

Aurora seemed quiet and composed when she reappeared and drank her tea. "A small piece of toast would be wonderful, Gran, thank you. I guess the day ahead is going to be a bit gruelling."

"The inspector will soon be here. I'm sure you'll find him very sympathetic. He's not one of those steely detectives you see on the telly. He's no fool, mind you, and knows instantly if someone is lying to him. But you know him anyway, don't you, from him being a regular customer an' that."

"Talk of the devil," said Gran. "That's him coming up the path. I'll let him in."

*　　*　　*

LOIS SAID SHE WOULD SEE COWGILL IN HER OFFICE. SHE WOULD go first, as she was a witness, too, and this would give Aurora time to prepare herself.

"He might as well see us together," said Aurora. "We both saw exactly the same thing."

"Police don't work like that," said Lois, and went through to welcome the inspector.

Seated in her office, Lois pointed to a chair on the other side of her desk. "You can sit here at my desk when you see Aurora, but for God's sake, be gentle with her. She has had a terrible shock."

"Of course. You know you don't have to tell me, Lois. I feel very sorry for the poor woman. It must have been a nightmare. Anyway, why don't you start from when you saw him last, in the bakery earlier on. I'll leave talking to Gran until last."

NINETEEN

❧

COWGILL WAS VERY PROFESSIONAL AS HE LISTENED TO LOIS'S account of yesterday's events. Lois could hear Jeems barking at a passing farmer's truck containing two sheep-dogs, known as the Enemy, and it did not seem possible that Aurora's husband, not such a bad chap but for his weakness with the ladies, had been drowned in such distressing cir-cumstances, while peaceful country life was going on as usual.

"Thanks, Lois," Cowgill said at last. "I'll be talking to you again, but for now perhaps you'd ask Mrs. Black to come in? She was very distressed when I talked to her yesterday, and I hope she may be feeling stronger today."

Aurora was pale but collected, and said in a small voice, "Good morning, Inspector." She sat down and folded her hands in her lap.

Cowgill said all the right things before asking her his first question. "Have you any idea, Mrs. Black, why your husband should be anywhere near the Mill House Hotel yesterday morning?"

She shook her head. "But we do know them all there so well, and we are always running across with extra bread for the restaurant, and things like that."

"The waterwheel is a magnificent piece of machinery. Was he particularly interested in it? I know that working mill wheels are difficult to find nowadays."

"Yes, he *was* fascinated by it, Inspector. He belonged to a sort of society of people who are interested in working mills, and so he knew very well how dangerous they could be. Of course, this wheel doesn't turn machinery anymore, and the hotel people keep it going as an added attraction. I know they were told to take all kinds of safety measures before they opened up the restaurant extension where the wheel can be seen turning. There had been some extra work going on, with those orange-striped cones all round a bit where they had taken the safety grid away. I can only think Donald ignored them, thinking he knew how to avoid the dangers."

Cowgill nodded. "And the last time you saw him was at home, in company with Mrs. Meade, who had called to see you?"

"Yes, that's right. And Lois and I were together the whole time from then on until I saw . . . well, until I saw Donald and screamed."

At this point, she slumped in her chair and closed her eyes, desperately trying to keep calm.

"Very well, Mrs. Black. That will be all for now. Do you plan to go back home today? I shall need to see you again, I'm afraid, as our enquiries proceed, but so long as you let us know if you are going away, that will be fine."

"Oh, I shall not be able to go away, Inspector. I have to get back to the bakery today. In fact, very soon. The bread won't wait for me, I'm afraid. The shop will be shut today, but open again tomorrow."

She almost smiled, and then walked calmly out of the office and back to the kitchen. "The inspector would like to see you now, Gran, if that's convenient," she said.

"Huh, or if it's not, I expect. Right, here goes. Help yourself to anything you fancy, Aurora. Shan't be long."

Lois made another cup of tea, and she and Aurora sat at the table in silence for a minute or two. Then Lois drew a deep breath and asked Aurora if she could think of any reason why Donald should have fallen into the water and been taken along by the flow across the wheel.

"Or was he pushed?" Aurora answered with a grim face. "I am sure that's what the police are thinking. Cowgill almost said it, but then skirted round it. And of course I've been thinking it myself. But he had no enemies, Lois. Always kind and charming to everybody. His cheerful personality was not put on, and it worked wonders in the jewellery parties. Only once have I known him to lose his temper with me, and that was when he shouted at you on the telephone! He apologised profusely afterwards."

"Was it something you said? I hope you don't think I'm prying, but my head is full of questions, as is yours, I'm sure."

"I can't really remember, but I think it was something to do with one of his colleagues. I thought he was trying to cheat Donald, but he wouldn't listen. He was very loyal to his staff. And that day he had a headache. I should have shut up!"

"Well, don't worry now. It'll turn out to have been a tragic accident, I am sure. Now, I am taking you back to the bakery, and I'll stay in case you feel wobbly."

"Thanks, Lois. You are such a good friend. Thanks for everything."

LOIS WAS NOT PRETENDING WHEN SHE SAID HER HEAD WAS FULL of questions, and some of them related to the previous death in the Mill House Hotel, including the woman who was found strangled with her own necklace. Donald Black had denied all likely connection with his jewellery business, though she had a collection in her bag.

When confronted with a photograph of the woman, he had said that he had never seen her before, and that she could have been one of the sellers recruited by someone else. Lois saw again the redhead under the potted palm. Was he being blackmailed by the murdered woman's friend? Or was it a romantic assignation? Or only a genuine business meeting, and the redhead one of his own recruits?

"The bread is proving now, Lois, and there is nothing more for us to do. Why don't you go off home, and then if you don't mind, we could talk on the telephone this evening. I expect it will all come flooding back—oh God! *Flooding!* Why does everything seem so watery this morning?"

She was in tears again, but sniffed them back and leaned forward to kiss Lois's cheek. "Off you go now. Safe journey home."

WHAT A BRAVE WOMAN! LOIS PUT HER VAN INTO GEAR AND drove slowly away, seeing in her driving mirror that Aurora was still watching and waving. And she was so efficient, as she prepared the dough for the oven! All kneaded by a steady hand, as if being punished for having the effrontery to rise, sometimes overspilling the tins. Perhaps it was a good way of releasing tension? Gran was a great one for vigorous cleaning and polishing, and she would say there was always plenty of tension in the Meade kitchen.

When she arrived home, she found washing blowing in the brisk wind, and Gran and her friend Joan up in the vegetable patch inspecting raspberry canes. Summer was well on the way now, and jam making in the offing. They were probably commiserating with each other over the cancelling of their plans, poor things.

There was a message for Lois in her office. Inspector Cowgill would be grateful if she could spare time to call in at the police station, if she was in town that afternoon. As it happened, she had planned to go in to the New Brooms office to have a couple of hours with Hazel going through paperwork. Hazel was very capable, but liked Lois to check in regularly.

She called his number. "About three? Is that okay? You won't be off to an important meeting the minute I arrive? I do have to get home to catch up on New Brooms matters. I cancelled my usual staff meeting today, and we'll be having it tomorrow at lunchtime. Has anything new come up?"

Cowgill said that he would save any developments until she called in. "Take care, now, Lois," he said. "Having too much on your mind can cause accidents. See you at three."

TWENTY

❧

HAZEL WAS PLEASED TO SEE LOIS, AS ALWAYS, AND ASKED about the family and Lois's friend Mrs. Black.

"She's still in shock, I think," Lois said. "Seems very calm and quiet, and carrying on the bakery on her own. I don't know what will happen about the jewellery business, though I know she helped Donald with it. She might decide to continue with it on her own, but it would be a lot of extra work."

"Have you bought any of the stuff? I went to one of his parties, and it was really nice. Very tasteful, but sparkly and nice, I thought."

"I bought a present for Josie. A real pearl, set as a pendant. I think my mum and her friend were thinking seriously of being Donald's sellers, setting up their own parties and so on. I think that's how it works."

"Would he have taken a percentage of what they sold?"

"No, they paid a membership fee, so they were members of the scheme. At their first party, they would get a starter pack at a big discount, and this was for demonstrations. Then they would take orders, and again take a cut as they sold the stuff. It's complicated, but I know there are incentives to get more and more recruits to sell jewellery. There were cleverly disguised things like having to find a set number of recruits in your first month of membership. After that, I'm not sure how it worked."

"You must have been a bit worried about your mother. Sounds like one of those notorious pyramid party ideas."

"Yeah, well, I think Donald must have found a legal way. He's been doing this scheme for some time, ever since he worked for the chiropodist. Fortunately, and according to my mother, no money had changed hands, except the membership fee, and that has a get-out clause."

Lois looked at Hazel, who was frowning. "And no, Hazel Thornbull! I did not drown him to extricate my mother from a crooked scam!"

Hazel laughed. "As if you would," she said.

"But someone did, unless he was in trouble, and jumped," said Lois, serious now. "Though for reasons unknown, at the moment. But the police are on to it."

They left the subject now and switched to New Brooms business. "There's a possible new client," said Hazel. "She phoned this morning. Lives over in Fletching, in a posh house by the river. I know it, from when John had a Prentise friend in the village. A Mrs. Prentise."

"Spelt with an *s*? It's an old Tresham name, but most people spell it with a *c*. I expect they get fed up with people getting it wrong. Well-known family in the seamier side of Tresham life. Go on."

"She said she was getting old and no longer able to keep the house as clean as she would like. I told her you would be in touch. Okay?"

Lois said she would go over tomorrow morning, so she would be able to sort out a rota for her with the others at the meeting.

After they were through with business matters, Lois asked if all was going well on the farm. Hazel's husband, John, was an old friend, and their little daughter one of Lois's god-daughters.

"John's very busy. He's bought new stock. A beautiful rare-breed bullock with curly hair, and a few heifers. You must come up and see them, Mrs. M. Any time. You're always welcome."

Lois thanked her, and gathered her papers together. "Better be off now. I have to call in at the police station at three, to be grilled by Inspector Cowgill on what I know about the Blacks. Not something I look forward to."

"Take care, then. See you later."

Inspector Cowgill was waiting in reception, and escorted her up to his office, where he sat down behind his desk and smiled broadly at her.

"What's new, then?" Lois said. "You look pleased with yourself this afternoon."

"You know perfectly well that you are the person I most

want to see at any time of day or night. But . . . First of all, how are you coping with Mrs. Black and her sad loss?"

"I'm all right, but poor Aurora is coping much too well."

"Meaning?"

"Meaning that she is quietly back into her usual routine in the bakery, and does not speak of the accident unless the subject is brought up by someone else. I suppose that's natural, but she looks like she's holding on tight and might give way any minute."

"Let me know if you need any help with her. She doesn't seem to have any helpful relations. No mother or sister. There is a daughter, I believe? Training to be a nurse? No, our Aurora's background is a bit of a puzzle. But she might like to talk about that to you? And then there's Donald. Neither of them seemed to have brought any friends or relations with them when they turned up in Brigham."

"I'll have a go. But first you can tell me something about that woman who was strangled in the hotel. What happened to the necklace? Does it go into a strongbox in the police station, or what?"

"Why do you ask? Do you want to see it? It is a valuable piece of evidence. I can probably get a photograph of it to show you, but I cannot allow you to keep it. The case is still very much open."

"I wouldn't ask if I didn't think it was important. I remember Donald saying they could order more of the same. Paperwork might be interesting, if this is the one ordered to replace Josie's. Customer's name, et cetera?"

"Best to find a photo now; then it won't leave the station."

Cowgill lifted his telephone and made a call. "It'll be here in a few minutes," he said. "There will be prints, of course."

They exchanged pleasantries about Josie and Matthew until a constable came in, bearing a folder with a photograph inside. Lois looked at it closely. It was a largish pearl, set into a slender silver chain.

"Oh dear," she said. "I think it's the same."

"Same as what?"

"Same as one I bought from Donald Black for Josie's birthday. Didn't you see it at that lunch we had in the hotel? I think she was wearing it then. She may be reluctant to keep it now, especially because it looks the same. Anyway, I don't suppose she is likely to see Sylvia's, or even this photograph."

The inspector took the photograph and looked at it for several seconds. Then he returned it to the folder. "Someone was very keen to silence poor Sylvia," he said.

TWENTY-ONE

✦

GRAN WOKE EARLY, AND AFTER WASHING AND DRESSING quietly, she went down to make herself an early cup of tea. She had planned to go round to see Joan mid-morning, so that they could privately work out how to retrieve their sizeable membership fees, already showing paid out of her bank account, and presumably Joan's, too. Now she needed to look for the documentation they had received from Brigham Jewellery, and then all would be well.

She found the folder they had been given by Donald and, to her chagrin, could find nothing relating to the membership fee. This was the first time she had really looked at the pieces of paper carefully. She had previously assumed anything Donald had given her would be bona fide.

"Mum? Are you all right?" It was Lois, standing in the

doorway in her dressing gown, rubbing her eyes. "You're up early, aren't you?"

Gran slid the folder under a cushion and said she had only woken up and thought she'd make an early start. "It's your New Brooms meeting at twelve, and I like to be ready to supply refreshments."

Lois knew this was an excuse. Her mother had been making trays of coffee and biscuits for the Brooms staff for several years now, and needed only about half an hour's notice.

"Why don't you go back to bed, and I'll bring you and Derek your cups of tea. By then it will be time for me to start on breakfast. Best smoked-back bacon with mushrooms this morning."

Lois frowned and shook her head. This was not the usual Gran. She was customarily full of doom and gloom at this time of the morning. She's hiding something, thought Lois. And I bet I know what it is.

"We'll be fine, thanks," she said. "I'll tell Derek about breakfast, and he'll be down like a shot." She smiled at her mother and disappeared upstairs.

Gran pulled out the folder, took it into the kitchen and put it in a large shopping bag, meaning to take it to Joan's. She had worried away a couple of hours before going to sleep last night, and in the end come to the conclusion that people don't get murdered for no reason. Donald Black was obviously up to no good with his mistress, and in Gran's book that made him untrustworthy. Before sleep finally came, she had decided she wanted no more to do with it, and would encourage Joan that the two of them should get out as soon as possible.

Between the two of them, they should be able to crack it. She supposed she should ask Derek for help, or even Lois, who, after all, ran her own business efficiently. Well, if all else failed, that is what she would do, and put up with the lectures and I-told-you-so's.

She turned up the Rayburn and began to heat the frying pan.

JOAN, MEANWHILE, HAD ANOTHER PLAN. SHE SUSPECTED THAT Donald was running a dodgy pyramid enterprise, and had been given a push into the mill water, where he would be drawn by the current approaching the mill wheel. Quite clever, really, she thought, as she washed her few breakfast dishes and swept the kitchen floor. And all cooked up by someone with a taste for the dramatic!

Next, a daily chore that she quite enjoyed. She had a beautiful ragdoll cat, and every day she brushed its fine long coat. This morning, the cat, named unimaginatively Hairy-puss, stood beside the heap of fur, meowing loudly for its saucer of milk, a reward for standing still as Joan brushed.

"There you are, then, puss," she said. "And there's Elsie coming down the passage, looking as if the end of the world is nigh!"

Gran waved through the kitchen window, and came on in, clutching her large bag, and steering well clear of the cat, which was inclined to make her sneeze.

"Morning, gel," she said. "I've come to get us sorted out. Are you ready?"

"I'm more than ready," said Joan. "I've thought of a master

plan, which will not only get us out of trouble with our nearest and dearest, but should make us a bit of pocket money on the side."

Gran stared at her. "It had better be good, Joanie," she said. "My only concern is to get our money back as soon as possible and hear no more, ever, about such plans. Are you going to get the kettle on? Sounds as if we shall need a coffee or two before we're finished."

When they were settled in Joan's comfortable sitting room, Gran said that she would set out what she planned to do, and then Joan could tell her about the fancy ideas she seemed to have dreamed up.

Joan agreed, smiled at the sarcasm, and told Gran to get going.

"Well, as you know, my Lois is working with the police on trying to find Donald's killer. If there was one. One of my guesses is that he had got himself in such a financial tangle that he jumped into the water, thinking someone would fish him out before he drowned and then he could confess why he'd done it and everybody would be sympathetic and helpful. We need to know if anyone was standing around and saw him jump."

"Maybe not, if he didn't get fished out in time?"

Gran nodded. "Got it in one," she said. "And then, there's the other possibility, that someone was there, and that same someone had a grudge against him and gave him a shove."

"Could he swim?" asked Joan.

"Dunno. Something else to find out. Lois knows his wife pretty well. We can get her to find out. You can bet the police have been on to that right away."

"So when we've found out all of this, how does it help us get our money back?"

Gran looked doubtful. "When we have all the information we need on who's behind this jewellery thing, we go straight there and demand our money back. There's bound to be money in the kitty somewhere. Now, can you do any better? I'm all ears."

"Right. First of all, we get our money back, minus a few pounds. We do this by finding out from Lois's friend Aurora who is taking over the jewellery business. I suspect she will do it herself. She must know all aspects of it off by heart, judging from the way she held the whole thing together that night when they did a party in Farnden. Then we get in touch and say we wish to remain in the scheme, but on our own terms."

"What d'you mean, on our own terms? You have to agree to the whole bit when you become a member."

"Ah, but that was in Donald's day. Now, say, it is Aurora. She will be only too pleased to listen to my plan, I am sure. We start in the same way, except we do it straight. That is, we give a thank-you fee to Aurora for putting us in touch with the suppliers, and then we buy direct from them. As extra inducement, we say we will give her a small cut on any future orders we produce. Then, we carry on as and when we feel like it. No new recruits. Just us. And thanks to the good old Women's Institute, we've both got enough savvy to do the organising, and a ready-made network of contacts to boot!"

Gran frowned. "I see a fly in the ointment," she said. "Supposing Aurora is not the boss, and the Blacks never have been? Suppose Donald was never top of the pyramid, never made the rules but just obeyed them?"

"Easy," said Joan. "We don't bother. It would be a bit of fun, but nothing else. We've both got enough to live on, and there's plenty of other things to do. A craft afternoon, for instance."

"And what craft were you thinking of taking up? I remember your last effort, Joan. A jersey with an ever-expanding neckline."

Joan began to laugh, and then Gran joined in, and they both agreed to meet again and never to take the whole thing too seriously.

"But we'll give it a go," Gran said, not wanting to hurt her friend's feelings. After all, Joan had given it a great deal of thought.

TWENTY-TWO

❧

IN HER MOTHER'S HOUSE, IN A BEDROOM STILL DECORATED with teenage rubbish, Gloria Prentise considered what she knew of her cousin's demise and that of her lover, Donald Black, who was indeed the boss of Brigham Luxury Jewellery. Her cousin, the woman found dead in bed in the hotel, the late Sylvia Fountain, had been one of his jewellery sellers as well as his well-established mistress. Sylvia's brother Peter acted as cover when she checked into the hotel, and then, after dark, Peter would leave, and Donald Black would creep into her bed for a spot of slap and tickle before dawn. As far as his wife was concerned, he had apparently given her a convincing explanation, using his out-of-town business trips as necessary fixtures.

Gloria knew all this from confidences exchanged with her cousin over a drink in the Purple Dog, and on occasion she had filled in entertaining a client when Sylvia was busy. Gloria was shattered at Sylvia's violent death and was determined to do all she could to find her killer.

She had tackled Donald on the day of the agricultural show and had tried a little gentle blackmail. For a small fee, she said she would keep quiet about him and Sylvia. They had been well shielded from public view, or so she thought, behind a potted palm and banks of flowers. He had dismissed her out of hand, and their meeting had ended acrimoniously. She had accused him directly of strangling her cousin—possibly in some gruesome game—and when it had gone too far, of legging it back home to Aurora. She had told him she had a friend at the cop shop who would be interested to hear her story.

Donald had refused to do anything but deny it, saying it was his word against hers, and who would listen to anything a carrot-headed whore had to say? Her threats were pure opportunism, and he had had no hesitation in saying his wife was behind him every step of the way.

Now he was dead, and Gloria was sitting in a café in Tresham, admitting to herself that she was frightened. She had loved her cousin Sylvia well, more as a sister. They had grown up together in the backstreets of Victorian terraces and scarcely ever ventured out of town. Until, that is, Donald Black had crossed their paths in a pub one night, and had fallen in an innocent way for Sylvia. She had made all the running, and had dreamed up the plan whereby they met regularly in the Mill House Hotel. The very proximity with his wife's bakery and her home had added spice to their relationship.

"Gloria Prentise! You look as if you'd lost a shilling and found sixpence! What's up, girl?"

It was Dot Nimmo, known to Gloria and her friends as the nosiest old nark in Tresham.

"Nothing at all, except a small hangover from a heavy session in the club."

"You should know better," Dot said, sitting down without being asked. "What's new in the seedier side of town?"

"Oh, get lost, Dot Nimmo!" Gloria said venomously.

"Missing your Sylvia?" said Dot. "If you take my advice, you'll make sure you don't end up the same way. I used to know your father, God rest his soul, and promised I'd keep an eye on you."

"Sod off," said Gloria, and pushing her chair back as she rose to her feet, she stalked off.

Dot chuckled. They were all the same, these poor kids. Started badly with the wrong crowd and never escaped. Still, she would keep her eye on Gloria, as promised, and might well be useful to Mrs. M at the same time.

Twenty-Three

Aurora Black awoke with a sense of optimism for the first time since the dreadful day of Donald's death. She had decided to continue the jewellery business herself, and had faced the fact that she would need some dogsbody help in the bakery. In order to set about this, she had drafted out an advertisement for the local paper, and would post it to the newspaper offices.

"Young assistant required," she had typed. "Interested in training in an old established bakery where bread, et cetera, is produced by hand in a traditional way. Apply to Brigham Bakery, telephone number, et cetera, et cetera."

That should attract the right sort of person, she reckoned. It could be boy or girl, of course. Or maybe neither! Working with floury hands in a tiny village in the countryside might not appeal. But, then again, the right person might well be looking for just such a job. She would see.

The shop bell rang, and with the advertisement in her hand, she walked through to find Lois smiling at her.

"Hi, Lois," she said. "You're earlier than usual. Will you have a coffee while I cool your loaves? You can check this for me." She handed over the draft and led the way into the room behind the shop.

Lois read the advertisement and nodded. "That's fine. If I didn't have New Brooms and ferretin' to take up all my time, I'd apply meself. You always look so serene and attached to the real things in life when you're working in your bakery."

"Not so sure about that! But you know you'd be welcome at any time to have a go at making your own bread. I could never understand why Donald never wanted to get floury hands . . . I suppose it wouldn't have done if he was called for an emergency dash to fit someone out with a diamond-encrusted tiara. Still, it suited me."

Lois smiled. "Do I sense a certain disapproval of the jewellery scheme? Would you rather he had stayed with the chiropodist?"

Aurora shook her head. "I don't know what happened about that. He came home with this scheme for selling jewellery, and that was that. He was a very private man, Lois. Kept his secrets close to his chest. I didn't mind, really, and when I was helping him with the parties, I got to know quite a lot about the business. Our two concerns dovetailed into each other quite nicely. I would make special tidbits to go with coffee at the parties, and help out with selling where necessary."

"So what are you going to do with it now? You must know pretty well every aspect of it. It sounds from this advertisement that you have made up your mind."

Aurora said that after a lot of thought, she had almost decided to give it a go. She would need extra help in the bakery for deliveries and other menial tasks. The actual baking she would keep for herself. Her customers expected her hand-baked bread to be made by her hands only!

"And who is going to help you with the jewellery parties? And no, I'm not offering the services of my mother and her friend Joan!"

"No need," said Aurora. "They've offered themselves." She smiled at the look on Lois's face, and said that so far she had not answered them. "They did very well at the agricultural show," she added.

"You didn't see how my mum flopped out on the sofa all evening! Still, we'll see, shall we? I'd appreciate it if you would keep me informed about Elsie and Joan."

"Certainly. Now, could you do me a favour, if you're going into town? I'm a bit stuck here. Could you drop this ad into the newspaper offices in the High Street, and then it should go into this week's classifieds."

Lois said she would be delighted. She had errands to run in Tresham, and it would be no trouble. "I do hope none of my girls think of giving bread making a try!"

Aurora smiled. "We workers must stick together, and I promise if any one of your Brooms girls applies for the job, I shall turn her down. How's that?"

"You're a brick. Now, is there anything else I can do for

you in town? I have to see Dot Nimmo, and probably Hunter Cowgill. But I'll still be around the High Street."

Aurora said the only brush she and Donald had had with the Nimmos had been to do with jewellery. "But the real thing, Lois. Some lovely stuff. Antique diamond rings, et cetera! Out of our league altogether."

"What's more," said Lois, "it had probably all been nicked! Must go. Bye, dear. Ring me any time."

DOT HAD BEEN ABOUT TO GO OUT WHEN LOIS HAD RUNG EARLIER this morning. "No, Mrs. M. Not a job. I was going to the supermarket. When did you want to come? Is it something urgent?"

"Sort of," said Lois. "How about eleven thirty?"

Now, thinking about it, Dot was puzzled. They had had the lunchtime meeting yesterday, and Mrs. M had not mentioned anything special. Still, if it needed confidentiality, she wouldn't have, would she? In any case, she herself had a lot to tell the boss.

She busied herself about the house, tidying up and cleaning areas where Mrs. M was likely to see. "Me job's cleaning," she said to the old parrot, "but I can do without a spotless house meself. And you're moulting, you disgusting old thing!"

Lois drew up outside Dot's house, and looked about. Not a soul, except for Hazel cleaning the office windows at the other end of the street.

"Come on in, Mrs. M," said Dot at the door. "Take no notice of the bird. I don't know why I don't give it its freedom."

Ann Purser

"Because it wouldn't last five minutes, that's why. Poor old thing. He's earned his retirement, hasn't he?"

Dot agreed that after her husband died, the bird was the only thing she had to tell how much she missed him. "Nimmos are supposed to be tough," she said. "No, I shall wait 'til I find him upside down in his cage; then I shall bury him in the back garden."

Lois felt an overwhelming desire to ask her if that's where she had buried her husband, but resisted it. "Yes, I'd love a coffee," she shouted, as Dot disappeared into the kitchen.

"So what's on your mind, Mrs. M?" They sat by the window, and Lois watched as the Tresham Zoo van drew up outside a house.

"Blacks, Aurora and Donald, that's what," said Lois. "I know I've asked you this before, but could you possibly either remember or discover anything else about them, particularly Donald? I know, of course, that Aurora has a daughter training to be a nurse. But Cowgill says they haven't yet built up a satisfactory picture of their lives, especially family contacts, and so on."

"I don't think I can get anything more from the Nimmo clan. And if they thought I was helping out the fuzz, they'd die of shock! So, no, not there. But as it happens, I do have something to tell you. Not exactly family, not in the sense you mean. But probably important."

"Come on, then, Dot, let's have it!"

"The woman found dead in bed in the Mill House Hotel? Yes? Well, she was Sylvia Fountain, of no fixed address, except a couple of rooms in the Purple Dog. Your friend Mrs. Tollervey-Jones, justice of the peace and hanging judge at the magistrate's court, she will probably have had her up before the bench more than once."

"Where are we going with this, Dot? I do have to see Cowgill sometime this morning."

Dot nodded. "You may not know that the very same Sylvia Fountain was the longtime mistress of the late Donald Black, of Brigham."

"What?!"

Dot took a deep, satisfied breath, and said that she thought Cowgill would reckon it was worth waiting for.

"But they questioned him closely. I'm sure of that."

"Oh, you'd be surprised how good these girls are at keeping their assignations secret. It is, after all, in their own interests. Sylvia used to check into the Mill House Hotel regularly with her brother Peter, supposedly for a quiet weekend. Then Peter was told to get lost, and Sylvia signalled the okay to a window in the bakery, and Donald slipped across the road like an overheated muffin!"

"Dot! What are you saying? How could he have done such a terrible thing to Aurora? She must have known. Oh Lord, poor thing. Why did she put up with him?"

"Perhaps he serviced her regular, too. Don't tell me I've shocked you, Mrs. M. I thought you were bombproof!"

"Oh, it's not the loose living, Dot. It is the disloyalty, the selfishness! He obviously didn't care two hoots, as long as he had his fun across the road." She looked at her watch. "I must be off to see Cowgill. Can I tell him all this? I don't want to get you into any trouble. I know the Nimmos still operate in the shadows in town."

"I think you'll find much of this comes as no surprise to

Hunter Cowgill," Dot said. "Just don't mention my name, if that's okay. But there is more, if you've got time."

"Heavens! Go on, then, Dot."

"Sylvia had a friend, a cousin, not to be dismissed lightly. I'm talking about a fellow worker, and she is pretty sore about the death of her cousin and colleague. I wouldn't trust her. I can't tell you any more at the moment, but should I overhear anything of use, I'll be in touch."

"Name?" said Lois.

Dot shook her head. Lois left quickly and headed for the police station and the newspaper offices.

TWENTY-FOUR

꩜

"COWGILL FIRST," LOIS SAID TO HERSELF, AS SHE DROVE INTO the car park at the back of the police station. She went quickly through to reception and came face-to-face with her son-in-law, Matthew.

"Lois!" he said. "Hello, Mother-in-Law. How are you?"

"Fine, thanks. How's Josie?"

"Very well, and looking forward to seeing you when you next call in to the shop. Are you here to see me, or the inspector?"

"Inspector Cowgill," said Lois, "who is coming down the stairs at this very moment. Nice to see you, Matthew."

After a few more pleasantries were exchanged, Lois followed Cowgill to his office. "I don't have much time," she said, as he held a chair for her. She had done some rapid thinking in her car, and decided to consider further whether she should tell him the sensitive information Dot had produced. Aurora had never hinted at such goings-on. It certainly increased the possibility of Donald having strangled his mistress in the hotel. He wouldn't have been the first man to find it necessary to get rid of an embarrassing association.

"Lovely as it is to see you, my Lois, do you have anything new and relevant to tell me? You're looking puzzled this morning."

Oh hell, she thought. "Well, I have just been to see Dot Nimmo, and she has told me the most extraordinary story about that woman who was strangled. She was apparently called Sylvia Fountain, which I'm sure you already know, but also she was a longtime mistress of Donald Black. Do you want the details?"

He nodded slowly. "That confirms it, then. We know she was selling his jewellery on the side, but could not trace any evidence that she had held parties. Not that sort, anyway."

A silence fell, whilst he looked at her, smiling fondly.

"Go on, then," she said.

"Tell me more," he said. "I have every respect for Dot Nimmo as a source of information, and you are much more likely to receive her confidences than I am. The Nimmos and the police are at permanent loggerheads."

"I can't believe it is as bad as that," Lois said. "Surely Tresham is a gang-free town? And from what I hear, the great days of the fearsome Nimmo gang are almost over."

"Almost," agreed Cowgill. "But there is a resurgence. A female whose name is Prentise. A cousin and big pal of Sylvia Fountain, and, I suspect, is behind several quite serious operations lately."

"Prentise? Sounds familiar. Does she have a Christian name?"

"Gloria. Flaming red hair. Some say glorious, but experts say it is all out of a bottle. She keeps a low profile, and so far we have not managed to pin anything on her. But we bide our time, Lois. As you know."

"Not any further forward, then, in the case of Donald Black? Could it be a revenge killing? Avenging the death of Sylvia? Hey, there could be a connection here!"

Cowgill raised his eyebrows. "Where?"

"Water," said Lois. "Sylvia *Fountain* and, in Donald's case, death by *drowning*."

Another silence. Then Cowgill frowned. "Are you serious, Lois?"

She stood up, laughing. "Of course not," she said. "Now, I must be going. Keep in touch."

Then she was gone, and he sat shaking his head and smiling. She was like a ray of sunshine in his somber day. How wonderful it would be if she brought sunlight to him every day of the week!

TWENTY-FIVE

࿊

LOIS WAS IN HER OFFICE, FACING A SMALL HEAP OF PAPER TO be gone through before coffee time. She had for many months now handed over the New Brooms wages, and other items of administration which did not need her, to Hazel in the office in Tresham.

The papers in front of her were confidential reports from her cleaning staff, and others from herself on potential clients who might need a follow-up. She began on the former, and was pleased with how smoothly everything seemed to be running. She loved especially the ones from Dot, which always had a humorous story or two to raise a smile.

Only one client was not yet signed up, and this was over at Fletching. Lois had been to call on the woman, who had grilled her thoroughly. After this, with no offers of cups of tea or general chat, Lois had left, convinced that this one was a no-go. But then yesterday there had been a message left for her, asking for another visit. Lois had begun to believe the woman was planning to set up a rival business, having learned all the details from New Brooms. It was a possibility.

She picked up the phone and dialled the Fletching number.

"Good morning, this is New Brooms. Lois Meade speaking. You left a message for me?"

The woman sounded much more friendly, and said she had decided to go ahead, and could Lois call in and they would discuss starting dates, et cetera.

Looking at the cleaning schedules, there seemed to be a spot for Floss to have time free. Mrs. Tolervey-Jones, unofficial assistant to Lois, and at present recovering from a serious illness, had insisted on retaining Floss as her New Brooms cleaner after she had moved from Farnden Hall to the Stone House in the village, but her hours had been cut. Mrs. T-J— as she was known by the cleaning girls—and Floss had always been a sympathetic pair, and Floss, keen on riding, regularly exercised the old mare that Mrs. T-J could not bear to sell. It lived a contented life in a small stable and coach house, disused for many years, that she had spruced up at the bottom of her garden.

Lois picked up her phone again, and dialled Floss. "Morning, all well?"

"Fine, thanks. About to go home. I've finished Mrs. T-J. Can I help?"

"Could you call in? I have another client for you. That is, if you can fit her in. I see you have Friday morning free at the moment. You can? Good. I'll pick you up tomorrow, and we'll go over to Fletching. I will introduce you, explain what's to be done, and then you can start next week. Okay?"

As Lois worked through the last of the reports, Gran stuck her head round the door and said she was going down to the shop, and then on to see Joan. Back in time to get lunch. Lois watched from her window as her mother walked briskly down the drive and disappeared. She's certainly got a spring in her step this morning, thought Lois. Ah well, Aurora had promised she would let her know what Gran and Joan were up to.

After she had tidied up her office, she set off upstairs to collect some washing and make sure Derek had not forgotten to change his vest. As she passed her mother's bedroom, she saw the door was open and a strong wind had got up and was blowing the curtains about. She walked in, closed the window, and was about to leave when she saw the wardrobe door was not quite shut and a large bag had been stuffed inside.

"What the hell is that?" she said aloud, and pulled the bag out so that she could push it in more tidily and shut the door. It was a strong canvas bag with a logo of a chrysanthemum flower entwining through a capital letter B. With great strength of character, knowing how furious her mother would be if she opened it, she returned it to its place in the wardrobe and shut the door.

The logo haunted her until Gran returned, and then, as Derek asked over his pudding if Lois knew how Aurora was doing, she knew what it was. Brigham Luxury Jewellery. So Elsie and Joan had got as far as a starter pack! And that would have been bought and paid for.

"Oh, all right, I think," she answered Derek. "Back in harness. With the bakery, anyway. I expect she has a lot of thinking to do before she can restart the jewellery business. What do you think, Mum?"

Gran went pink, cleared her throat and said there was more pudding if anyone wanted seconds.

TWENTY-SIX

FLOSS WAS ALREADY PARKED OUTSIDE BRIAR HOUSE WHEN Lois arrived next morning. Lois beckoned to her to come and sit with her for a few minutes, while she briefed her on what they knew so far on the new client.

"I don't know her Christian name," said Floss, "but I remember she donated to charity the proceeds of opening her garden one year."

As they walked up the short drive to the house, Lois looked around and said it was certainly a lovely garden. "She must be loaded to hire a gardener to do all of this. Looks like it's been trimmed with manicure scissors!"

"What's her name, Mrs. M? I'd better know it, if I'm going to work here."

"Um, hang on. I'm showing my age, Floss, when I can't remember names! No, I've got it. Mrs. Diana Prentise. I knew I'd heard it somewhere before! She's lived here some while now, but originates from Tresham. Very pleasant on the phone, the second time she rang. Ah, I think someone's coming."

They were given coffee, and invited to sit in a long, low-ceilinged room, where heavy black beams supported the ceiling like the backbones of a flatfish.

Lois opened the conversation, and then handed it over to Floss. Mrs. Prentise offered to show them over the house, and it was when they were ushered into a pink, overfrilled bedroom that Lois remembered where she had heard the name previously. Gloria Prentise, of course.

"Do you have a daughter?" she said. "This is such a lovely girl's room."

"It was my daughter's, a long time ago now. But she occasionally spends the odd night or two here and likes me to keep the room as it was."

Lois looked at her more closely. Her hair was a uniform grey, with no signs of having once been red. She was neat and expensively dressed, guessed Lois. That kind of muted elegance costs money. Perhaps she had been on the game until retirement, with her daughter following in her footsteps?

Her thoughts were interrupted by a sudden burst of laughter from Floss. She and Mrs. Prentise had gone on ahead, so Lois caught up and asked what had been so funny.

"That black furry monkey!" said Floss, pointing out of the window at a rose-covered brick wall in the garden. "It's a toy, look, see how it is holding on to a stem with its hands and dangling its feet below." She laughed again, and Mrs.

Prentise smiled. "My daughter calls him Black Jack! Don't ask me why. He stays out there, come rain or come shine, without deteriorating. Now, you go downstairs first, Floss. I am so old now that I often trip up."

Lois followed behind the other two, and wondered at the warped sense of humour that could hang like a biblical criminal on a rosy crucifix, an innocent toy. Still, it had amused Floss, so she supposed it wasn't all bad.

Lois answered a few more questions about cleaning schedules, and added details of New Brooms prices. Mrs. Prentise waved that aside, saying she was glad to be able to support her old age in the manner to which she had been accustomed.

Lucky you! Lois was beginning to dislike this smug old woman, and then unbidden a thought came into her head. Wouldn't she be a likely candidate for one of Gran and Joan's jewellery parties? Then she remembered she thoroughly disapproved of those, and somewhat abruptly ushered Floss out of the front door, saying that, if convenient, New Brooms would start in a week's time.

"You didn't like her, Mrs. M, did you?" said Floss, as they drove away.

"I don't have to like the clients, and nor do you, Flossie dear," said Lois. "We just go in and do a job as well as possible, and that's it. I'll say what I always say, as you know; be on your guard and report back to me anything untoward that is said or heard by you whilst you are working there."

Floss frowned. "I don't think I've heard you say it quite so seriously before. Do you know something about Mrs. Prentise that perhaps I should know, too?"

"We have a week before you start. Then you'll either be fine there, or withdrawn."

Then Lois changed the subject, and asked Floss how her parents were, and had she decided where to go on holiday this year?

"I SHALL BE GOING ROUND TO JOAN'S THIS AFTERNOON," SAID Gran, as she dished up shepherd's pie for lunch. Derek had come home, as he was working nearby, and he was half listening to Gran when Lois suddenly blurted out that if Gran and Joan did not stop this nonsense she would have to do something about it.

"For heaven's sake, Lois," he said. "Your mother and Joan can do what they like with their own money, so long as nobody gets hurt in the process."

"That's exactly it," said Lois, remembering the starter pack in Gran's wardrobe. "I have this nagging feeling that not only them but other suckers might get hurt! Anyway, I am going to see Aurora this afternoon, so I shall ask her what exactly is happening with the jewellery scam."

Gran stood up, crashing her chair backward. "Lois Weedon!" she said loudly. "It is not a scam! It is, as Derek says, my money. I like the idea of running a little business on the side, and you can trust me not to break the law, for God's sake! And as for Aurora Black, you should remember that she is mourning a partner, and the last thing she needs is you going in there insulting her husband's profession!"

"Profession? I don't call it a profession running a dodgy business like he did."

"It is *not* dodgy!" shouted Gran. "And I'll thank you to mind your own business for once!"

Gran walked towards the door. "And you keep away from that inspector! I'll not put up with it; so there!"

Derek rested his elbows on the table and put his head in his hands. "God save us," he muttered.

"What did you say?" Lois was still steaming.

"I said, God preserve me from women. That's all. Now, are you going to make us a cup of coffee before I get back to work to keep us all with a roof over our heads?"

TWENTY-SEVEN

❧

J OAN WAS WAITING AT HER DOOR, AND KNEW FROM THE LOOK
on Gran's face that something was wrong.

"Come on in, Elsie," she said. "And you can tell me what's
up. Has your Lois been getting at you again?"

Gran was immediately on the defensive. Nobody was
allowed to criticize any member of her family but herself. "I
suppose she thinks she's doing the best for her silly old
mother," she said. "I have reservations; of course I have. Both
of us were taken for a bit of a ride. But we shall be more careful now, and make a success of it. Then Lois will be proud
of us."

"That's the spirit," said Joan. "Now, sit down at the table,
and I'll show you what I've prepared."

She spread out a large sheet of paper, with her name and
Gran's written at the top. Then, in the well-known pyramid

shape, she had drawn tentacles reaching from two each down to a row of question marks.

"What's them marks for?" Gran asked.

"Well, they mean we can stop whenever we like. We just close down the jewellery supply. Foolproof."

"So they buy all the jewellery from us? Sending us orders and then we take a cut on all, then they take a cut, and so on and on?"

"And we are the only ones who actually supply the starter pack—which they pay for—and any forthcoming orders."

Gran was silent for a moment. Then she said she could see one major fly in the ointment. "I bet you it dries up sooner than you think," she added. "There just aren't that many willing sellers around here. And anyway, after a couple of parties, people will have got all the jewellery they need."

"That can happen," agreed Joan. "But by the time we've got about eight people selling, we'll encourage them to spread the net wider. Ask friends and relations from farther afield. It works with other schemes."

Huh, thought Gran. The scheme sounded very like Lois's warning of scams! "And another thing," said Gran. "You and I now have our starter pack, which we've paid for, but we'll need more money to buy our first lot to sell. If we sell our starter pack, we'll have nothing to demonstrate with."

"I've thought of that," said Joan proudly. "We sell some of it, but have some photographs enlarged to demonstrate the rest. More than we could do with stuff actually on the table. Then, as we take orders, we'll be able to be flexible."

"It costs money to have professional photographs enlarged," said Gran doubtfully.

"The jewellery suppliers can take care of that, I'm sure," said Joan. She was beginning to wonder if Gran's heart was still in it. That wretched daughter of hers has been putting the boot in; that was obvious.

"Is that all, then, Elsie?" she said. "Shall I make us a cuppa? Then we can do some party planning." She disappeared into her kitchen, and Gran sat staring at the pyramid. Joan was her best friend, and always straight and clever with it. And it would be wonderful if they made it work. Joan still drove, and could take them to village halls and reading rooms to find the best locations for their parties, and they would meet nice new people. She was so dug into Farnden village life that she sometimes longed to be somewhere else, someone else.

She had lived with Lois for years now, and inevitably her personal life had been absorbed into the general family goings-on. She did her best, with membership in the Women's Institute and the occasional day out with Joan. She went to church regularly, but on the whole found her fellow worshippers snooty and elitist, as if going to church made them superior.

No, this would be hers alone. Well, hers and Joan's. If they made a mess of it, then too bad. At least they would have tried and got their brains working again!

"Do you want a hand, Joan?" she called, and went out into the kitchen.

"Let's get another sheet of paper," Joan said, "and we can make a list of people to ask and where to have it. I think our first party should be fairly local, but in a smaller venue, as Donald had already collared the market round here."

Impressed by Joan's mastery of the jargon, Gran said why not the Reading Room in Fletching? It had recently been restored and had kitchen facilities. Everything was clean and new, and just the job for a jewellery party.

"One thing you haven't asked me," Joan said, offering a plate of Jaffa Cakes to Gran. "Where do we get the jewellers who will agree to our terms, instead of the other way round?"

"Ah, now I might be able to help there," said Gran, who was beginning to feel much the weaker partner in this enterprise. "When I lived in Tresham, my next-door neighbour had a jewellers shop in town. It wasn't in the posh part, but very central, and when they'd got a reputation for good stuff sold at reasonable prices, the word got round, and they did very well. I was quite close to the wife at that time, and I could certainly get in touch and put a proposition to her."

Joan clapped her hands in delight. "Wonderful, Elsie. So now we're all set. You see your friend in town, and I'll go to Fletching to book the Reading Room."

"And I'll make a list of all the friends I used to have in Tresham who might like a trip out to Fletching and take in a jewellery party. What time shall we have it? I suggest half past six in the evening. It's light until late now, so it couldn't be better for us."

"And what about that starter pack?" said Joan. "Do we sell it?"

Gran shook her head. "Send it back. If I set up a deal with the jewellers in Tresham, they won't want us selling someone else's stuff. And that business we agreed to, about having however many parties a month it was, will be null and void."

"Elsie! You're a wonder!"

Gran nodded, and said she'd better be getting back home before Lois came after her with the handcuffs.

TWENTY-EIGHT

❧

"ARE YOU GOING INTO MARKET AT TRESHAM TODAY, LOIS? Saturday market is always the best."

Gran had been thinking. She would get a lift into town with Lois, and then go off on her own to find the jewellers.

"I thought I'd look up some people I used to know up on the Mounts. That district has definitely come up in the world, and I should think they do well. They always send me a Christmas card, and it would be nice to see them again. I'll get the bus home. I'll enjoy that, and I've got my old people's bus pass."

"Itchy feet, Mum?" said Lois. She had thought long and hard about her row with Gran, and decided she would try to understand her a little better. Perhaps they did take her too much for granted.

"No, of course not. I don't have to account for my every move, do I?"

"Let's have no more of that," said Derek, from behind his sports pages. "Little birds in their nests agree. Never a truer saying than that."

"And what about the cuckoo's eggs laid in other birds' nests? The little cuckoo hatches and shoves the rest out to die on the ground!"

Derek rose to his feet, scratching his head. "I give up," he said. "See you at lunchtime, me duck, and you'd better ring us, Gran, if you miss the bus home. There's only the one."

"Okay, then, Mum. Can you be ready in half an hour or so? I want to go over to Brigham to see Aurora later. See how she is. I might be able to help."

THE MORNING MARKET WAS BUSY AND LIVELY AS ALWAYS. A busker with a pennywhistle was playing at one corner, and his girlfriend sang along every now and then. They were good, and Lois stopped to listen and put money in the straw boater upturned on the ground in front of them.

"My lucky day," said a familiar voice behind her, and she turned to see Hunter Cowgill. "Hello, Mrs. Meade," he said. "Shall we dance?"

"Have you been drinking, Cowgill?" said Lois irritably.

"Certainly not. I need no extra stimulant when there's a chance I might see my favourite sleuth around the market. You usually come here on Saturdays. But where's your mother? Mrs. Weedon gets a lift in most weeks, doesn't she?"

"Yes, she does, and thereby hangs a tale. This week she came in with me as usual, and instead of us going around the market together, she told me some trumped-up story about visiting a friend on the Mounts, and disappeared before I could argue."

"No wonder you are a little tetchy, my dear," he said. "But I am sure she will be fine. After all, she lived in Tresham for many years. Since her birth, I believe? She's bound to know her way around."

"I know, but she's never bothered about these mythical friends before. She and that Joan friend of hers are up to no good. Not your sort of no good, of course. But they've been hooked by the idea of pyramid selling of some sort, and they are a real gullible pair!"

"What? Your mother gullible? I would not agree with that, Lois dear. Anyway, now you've told me, I'll bear it in mind and keep an eye on things. Now, how about a drink with me in our usual café?"

Lois sighed. "Go on, then," she said. "I'll tell you what I know so far. Mum's getting the midday bus back. She insisted, so it means I shan't see her until about half past twelve."

"I am sure she will return full of news from her old friends."

"As long as she returns, I don't care what she tells us. If she and Joan are really going ahead with their plan, I mean to check on her every move. I know that the Brigham jewellery is basically rubbish, but the word might well get round that the two old ducks are pottering about with bags full of jewels and money. You know what villages are like!"

"You may be right, Lois. Would you like me to have a

word with your mother? Now I am family, however remotely, she might listen to me."

"Not at the moment, thanks. I'm hoping to see Aurora Black this afternoon. I mean to go over to the bakery and see if she has anything to report on Mum and Joan."

They finished their coffee and walked out into the market. Everything looked bright and normal, and Cowgill disappeared to return to the station. Lois wandered round, her mind not really on her shopping list. Then she nearly jumped out of her skin when she felt a hand on her arm.

"Here I am," said Gran. "I hoped I'd catch you, and there'd be no need for me to catch the bus."

"But what about your f-f-friends?" stammered Lois.

"The one I wanted to see wasn't there, so I'll go back another time. Probably best to ring first."

Feeling ridiculously relieved, Lois took hold of her mother's arm and said she wanted to show her a pair of slippers that she might like as an unbirthday present. Gran, astonished by this, said she would have to go missing more often. The slippers were approved and stashed away in a bag, and mother and daughter returned to the car and set off back to Long Farnden.

TWENTY-NINE

❧

LUNCHTIME CAME, AND AS DEREK, LOIS AND GRAN SAT down to eat, a shadow passed by the window and Josie appeared at the door.

"Guess what?" she said.

"What?" chorused Derek and Lois.

"We have a new shop assistant. Matthew, my off-duty policeman husband, suggested he take over for an hour to allow me to visit my aged relatives in Meade House."

Derek laughed. "You're pulling our legs," he said. "You've got Floss in, to give you a break."

"No, honest, it is true. He offered. God knows whether he is capable, but I thought at least if he had cheeky chappies or belligerent customers to deal with, he would know exactly what to do. Worth a try, don't you think, Mum?"

"I don't see why not," said Lois. "Sit down over there, and have a sausage or three. Veg in that dish. Derek, pass her the mustard. Plenty of everything, thanks to your Gran."

"Any news, Mum, on the dreadful mill-wheel murder? And before you correct me, I know there's no proof that it was murder, but every customer in the shop is convinced it was. The general consensus is that Donald Black had made enemies way back. He's had a number of different enterprises, apparently, and not all squeaky clean."

"Perhaps you'd like me to ask Aurora. I am going to see her this afternoon, and I could question her about her late husband's squeaky-clean ventures." Her voice was ice-cold, and Josie frowned.

"Don't take it seriously, Mum. You know it's only gossip in the village shop. That's what most people come in for! And, as you know, I keep quiet and listen. It wouldn't do for me to take sides."

"Why don't we change the subject?" said Derek. "I'm fed up with hearing tittle-tattle. The strangled woman is nothing to do with us, and the police will know if there was a link with the jewellery bloke. End of story. Now, tell us, Josie, how you're getting on with the gardening, you and Matthew? I've got some radish seed left over. Would you like it?"

The conversation limped on, with Lois obviously regarding radishes as unimportant and Derek refusing to let her quiz Josie on what she had heard on either the woman strangled in the hotel or Donald Black spread-eagled on the dripping waterwheel.

*   *   *

AURORA WAS SERVING IN HER SHOP WHEN LOIS ARRIVED. A fresh-faced, plump woman loaded up her bag with bread and wished Aurora a cheery goodbye.

"Hi, Lois! Lovely to see you. Have you got time for a chat? Most of my weekend customers have been in now, and I have very little bread left. There's a large white, and four soft rolls, if you'd like them."

Lois accepted the bread and said she had really come over for a chat, if Aurora had time. They made sure the bell over the door was working and retired to the sitting room behind the shop.

"I'm glad you came over today," Aurora said. "Some good news to report. At least, I hope you'll think it good news, and I did for your sake."

"They've found the truth of what happened to Donald?" said Lois anxiously.

Aurora shook her head. "No, I had a visitor about half past nine this morning, and could not believe my eyes when I saw Joan Whatsit—you know, Gran's friend—struggling out of her car and into the shop with two heavy canvas bags. Brigham Jewellery bags! Seems these starter packs had been delivered to Gran and Joan, paid for, and were now returned to me as they had decided not to go ahead with our scheme! I remembered what you asked me to do, Lois, and so I am now reporting that they are completely unconnected with our jewellery."

"Thank the Lord for that," said Lois. She almost asked

Aurora if she would give the two their money back, but thought it would seem a bit ungracious, when there was probably a no-return clause in the scheme.

"I shall certainly return their payments," Aurora said, mind reading. "We don't usually, but it is the least I can do in return for all your kindness."

Lois leaned forward and patted her arm. "You're a star, Aurora," she said. "I can't tell you how relieved I am, and I know they'll be grateful, too. I think it was my mum's fault, getting carried away with the glamour of running a jewellery business!"

"It is far from glamorous," said Aurora. "There's an awful lot of work involved. Sometimes Donald would come back from one of his selling trips absolutely exhausted."

And I know why, thought Lois. But she said, "And what about you? How are you going to manage two businesses at once?"

Aurora smiled. "Ah ha! Let me show you my secret weapon!"

She walked to the foot of the stairs and called. "Milly? Can you come down for a second?"

This was followed by light steps, and a girl with long, jet-black hair stood before them, smiling fondly at Aurora.

"This is my daughter, Milly," Aurora said. "She has decided to take a year off from her nursing to help me pull things together. I am so pleased, as you can imagine, Lois. Perhaps we can get our daughters together? Lois's daughter, Josie, runs Farnden Village Shop, Milly, and is married to a policeman."

"I'd love to meet her," Milly said. "At the moment I am

trying to help Mum as much as possible, so we can come to terms with my father's shocking death. Have you known us long, Mrs., er . . . ?"

"Meade," said Lois. "Long enough to admire your mother's courage and determination," she said.

The girl disappeared back upstairs, and Aurora smiled proudly. "Lovely, isn't she?" she said. "It will be great to have her help, though I am determined she shall go back to nursing after a year. By then, I shall be firmly settled, and I might even take a short holiday! Do you fancy a girls' weekend away, Lois?"

"Sounds nice, but not at the moment. Maybe later." She nearly said that she had a husband who would want to be with her if they had time to spare, but remembered in time. It was going to be difficult for quite a while not to be cruel or tactless, but she trusted Aurora would know no hurt was intended.

THIRTY

෴

IN TRESHAM, IN A STREET LINED WITH TERRACES OF BRICK
houses and the occasional small shop, a woman stood at
her open doorway, talking to her next-door neighbour.

"Did you say Elsie Weedon came calling yesterday?
Haven't seen her for years."

"Nor had I, but I remembered her the minute I set eyes
on her. She hasn't changed one iota. Same eyes everywhere,
same sharp voice. But she was very friendly and wanted to
have a chat about our jewellery business. I couldn't think
why she should want to do that. After all, she must be getting on."

"Perhaps she was mixed up. They get like that. Old
people. Always wandering off and getting lost."

"She wasn't confused; I'm sure of that. Anyway, I told
her Ted would help her when he came back. He's been away

up London for a few days, as you know. Hatton Garden, buying a few nice pieces. We like to keep up our standards!"

"So she'll be calling again? Let me know when she does. I'd like to take a look at her. She was a bit of a dragon in the old days!"

Joan, meanwhile, knowing that Elsie had gone into town to see her jeweller friends, had driven on from Brigham to do a small tour of the villages, looking out for attractive village halls and shops where she could leave notices once they got going with parties.

This had taken up most of the morning, and she ended up in Fletching, where she noted down the booking details. She was on the lookout for halls where the Women's Institute had a branch. She knew they had monthly meetings, and from her own time of being secretary in Long Farnden, she also knew it was a struggle finding interesting speakers or demonstrators.

As she finally got into her car to return home, she realised they would need a snappy name for the business. *Joan 'n' Elsie?* Lord no. *Farnden Sparkles?* Rubbish. Maybe Elsie would have some ideas, but the sooner they got on with it, the better. She decided to give her a ring when she got home and invite her round for supper.

"Did you do well?" said Josie, as Matthew came in after shutting up the shop. "I hope there's no rules about policemen running a village shop on the side."

"No, but I am very glad I had a session in there. My good-ness, you really hear some useful info on local goings-on!"

"So what's the latest? I'm surprised people were talking when you were behind the counter. I know you're not in uniform, but everyone knows you're a copper."

"They also know I am a useful chap to have around. But the latest item on the agenda seemed to be a mugging. In fact, two muggings. One in Fletching and one in Brigham."

"Heavens! What happened? Have you caught the mugger?"

"Give us a chance, Josie! These two attempts to steal money and so on took place in broad daylight yesterday. Nobody about in these villages, especially ones without a pub or a shop."

"Or school," said Josie. "Schools bring life to a village. We're lucky in Farnden. Anyway, did he get away with anything?"

"Yes, I'm afraid so. In each case, a man approached an elderly woman and asked for change for a phone call. When their handbags were open, he lifted the lot, and in one case, also a packet of tranquilizing drugs, on prescription and just collected from the chemist."

"Nasty," Josie said. "But neither were hurt, were they?"

"Not hurt, but badly frightened. One of the victims has a bad heart, and she was the one who had the sense to send a message to us at the station. I am going over there shortly, to collect some details."

"Did they get a description?"

"Yes, and both said more or less the same thing. A tall youth, nice smile and bad teeth."

"Not much to go on, then. Anyway, I'll put up a notice in the shop on Monday, if you haven't got him by then."

"Thanks, love. Meanwhile, we'd better warn our Gran not to speak to any tall youths with bad teeth. And certainly not to open her handbag."

"Now you've frightened me! Is she likely to be approached by him?"

"Probably not. He's more than likely some chancer who's got wheels and motors round an area and then moves on. There's a gang of them in Tresham, all linked to the old rotten lot who imagined themselves members of a film-style baddies' world. They're like young students learning an illegal trade, whatever is current. Lately, it seems to be mugging old ladies. The lads do any dirty work that's going, so the real criminals are hard for the police to pin down. No, don't alarm her, but a gentle warning would be a good idea."

MEANWHILE, UNAWARE OF ANY DANGER, GRAN ANNOUNCED her intention of walking round to Joan's for supper. "I've left a casserole in the oven for you two," she said. "I suppose I'll be back around nineish, but if I'm late, don't wait up. I'll let myself in and lock up as usual."

"What's with you and Joan lately?" said Lois. "You're always in each other's pockets. I don't like the idea of you walking back in the dark."

"It'll not be dark, not properly. And anyway, I could walk from Joan's to here blindfold. Shall I take Jeems and give her a bit of an airing? Joan always loves to see her."

"Good idea," said Derek. "Sharp little teeth could do a lot of damage. The dog's, I mean, Gran."

"Ha ha," said Gran. "So I'll be off now. Come on, Jemima dog; let's be going."

Shortly after she had gone, with Jeems willingly accompanying her, the phone rang. "Let it ring," said Derek. "It'll only be Dot Nimmo with a complaint."

"Hello?" said Lois. "Oh, it's you, Dot. Derek must be psychic. No, he hasn't been to the doctor. How can I help?"

Dot asked Lois if she had seen the local television news. "There's this mugging merchant, specialising in old ladies."

"So you immediately thought of me?"

"No, no, Mrs. M. I thought of your mother, but I expect she's seen the news. She's just the sort of well-heeled-looking older woman that he's approaching. He asks for money to make a phone call, and when they open their bags, he's in there, scooping out the contents. And then he's off like the wind."

"On foot?"

"Yeah—but they reckon he's got some sort of transport parked round the corner. I've had the word from my illustrious family. Although I have nothing to do with them anymore, they keep an eye on me for my dear husband's sake. Useful, sometimes. I thought of Mrs. Weedon, because there has been some gossip going round, saying she and her friend are taking over that jewellery business at Brigham. You know, the one that bloke ran before he got murdered."

"How on earth did that gossip get round? Of course my mum is not taking over. She's an elderly woman, with no experience of running a business! I don't know how these stories start, but you could scotch that one if you hear it again."

Lois thanked Dot for ringing, and stared at Derek. "We told her, didn't we, that she should be careful. Thank goodness she took Jeems. Perhaps you should go round later and escort her back home?"

Derek shook his head. "Can you imagine what she would say? No, we'll have to trust she would be sensible and keep walking. They say a terrier is the best antiburglar protection."

At around nine o'clock, Lois looked at her watch and said wasn't it time Gran returned? Derek told her not to stew. "She's a sensible woman, and it is still daylight outside. Look out there. There's old Jim going down to the pub, and there's still kids playing outside."

By ten o'clock, Lois said she was going to ring Joan and tell her that she was coming round to walk Mum back home. She wanted a breath of fresh air before bedtime, she said. Before she could reach the telephone, Derek stopped her.

"Listen!" he said. "What's that noise outside the back door? That'll be her returning. So, no need to worry, me duck. I'll go and let her in. Maybe she's forgotten her key."

He went off to the kitchen, and then Lois heard him call. "Elsie? Come on in, dear."

Lois walked quickly through, and saw to her horror that Jeems, usually so clean and fluffy, was muddy and wet, and had rushed straight into her basket where she lay whimpering.

There was no sign of Gran, in spite of Derek calling and calling at the top of his voice.

Thirty-One

༄

Wᴉᴛʜ ᴀʟʟ ᴛʜᴇ ᴏᴜᴛsɪᴅᴇ ʟɪɢʜᴛs sᴡɪᴛᴄʜᴇᴅ ᴏɴ, Dᴇʀᴇᴋ and Lois searched and called all around the garden, in case Gran had fallen and not been able to get up again.

"No sign. Lois, you go in and ring Joan, and then we'll look down the road, and then it's PC son-in-law to help."

Lois disappeared inside the house, only to reappear in minutes to say that Gran had left Joan and set off with Jeems about a quarter of an hour ago. It was a ten-minute walk, and so she must have stopped off somewhere between there and Meade House.

Armed with torches, Lois and Derek set off. They agreed they would not take Jeems, as she was in a terrified state already. There were no streetlights, except for the one over the shop, and as they went they called out, especially along by a piece of rough ground between the shop and the side road that led to Joan's house. They were just nearing the end of a ruined cottage when Lois stopped suddenly.

"Derek! Hush! Did you hear that? I am sure I heard a sound. You call really loudly!"

Derek yelled "Elsie! Gran!" at the top of his voice, and at last there was a weak shout.

"Over here . . . I'm over here."

Avoiding brambles and piles of old bricks, they made their way towards the voice. It was Gran, half sitting, half lying, on a bare patch of ground. Lois rushed towards her and put her arms around the shaking shoulders.

"What took you so long?" Gran said finally. "I should have thought you would at least have got the police dogs out looking for me."

Derek snorted. "That's all we get for scratched legs and stubbed toes! Come on, you old battle-axe, up we get."

He hauled her to her feet, and realised that for all her brave face, she was actually shaking from head to foot. "Hold on tight to me," he said, and lifted her into his arms. Stepping slowly over sundry obstacles, they reached the path.

"Put me down now, Derek. I'll be fine. Let's get back home. Did Jeems come and find you? I sent her off to tell you I needed help."

They said that yes, Jeems had raised the alarm. "We must give her some warm milk and get the mud off her coat." Lois added that they should have no more talking until they were safely back home, when Gran could tell them exactly what happened.

*   *   *

ALTHOUGH IT WAS SUMMER, THE NIGHTS LATELY HAD BEEN VERY cold, with a north wind sweeping down the street and making it seem more like autumn. By the time the trio reached home, even though Derek had put his jacket round Gran's shoulders, they were all in dire need of a hot drink.

"Tea for me, please," said Gran, as Lois sat her down by the Rayburn and wrapped her round with a warm shawl.

"And a slug of this in it," said Derek, wielding a bottle.

When they were all settled, Lois suggested it was time for Gran to tell them what had happened.

"Well, to begin at the beginning, I had had a nice evening with Joan, and I stayed to watch the end of that detective series on the telly. I set off with my torch and Jeems on her lead, and as I came up to that rough ground, I heard a car coming up behind me. I think I turned to wave him off, but the headlights were on, and he just kept coming. There's a deep muddy puddle just there, and I'm sure he deliberately sent great showers all over me and Jeems. Jeems pulled at the lead, and I ran towards that opening in the wall and kept running."

"What about the car?" Derek put another slug into Gran's mug.

"He must have swerved away at the last minute," she said. "By that time, I had dropped my torch, and it was complete darkness. I stumbled around for a bit, then tripped and fell where you found me. I sent Jeems off up to home, and hoped you would see her outside the back door."

"Which we did," said Lois. "What a horrible time you've

had, Mum. I'm going to phone Joan to say we've found you, and tell her briefly what happened."

"Don't make too much of it, Lois. I don't want her to think I'm a silly old woman who can't find her way back home."

After a hot bath with lots of fragrant bath essence, Gran finally went to bed and fell instantly into a deep sleep. Lois and Derek stayed behind in the kitchen for another half hour, turning over what she had said.

"One thing I noticed," said Lois. "Mum always said 'he' did this and that. You can't actually see the driver when the headlights are dazzling you. It could equally well have been a woman, don't you think?"

Derek nodded. "So you don't think it was the thieving mugger?"

"He would hardly have nearly run her over if he wanted to encourage her to open her handbag for him, would he? And anyway, he has always acted in daylight so far."

"True. Do you have any other idea? You've got that sleuthy look in your eye. For God's sake, let's get it out in the open and put a stop to all this nonsense."

Lois stared at him. "I don't think it's anything to do with those other muggings. I expect it was some idiot having what he would think was a bit of fun. Scaring old ladies would appeal to some. Other than that, I think he must have come too fast round the bend there, and lost control of the car. Then, having seen Mum disappearing through a hole in the wall, he scarpered."

"I dunno. I'm out of my depth, Lois dear. Let's go to bed."

THIRTY-TWO

꒰

L OIS WAS FINDING IT DIFFICULT TO CONCENTRATE ON THE business of New Brooms with the team of cleaners arriving for their weekly meeting. She could not escape a replay of finding her elderly mother in a state of collapse in the dark on muddy ground. She finally snapped to attention when Dot Nimmo said loudly, "Mrs. M, is there something wrong?" It was always Dot who dared to ask what the others were thinking.

"Oh, sorry, Dot, and everybody. It's just that my mother had a bit of an accident yesterday. She's fine, as I'm sure you gathered when she let you in! But you know how it is with not-so-young people."

"Nice way of putting it, Lois," said a voice from the hall. The office door had been left ajar, and Gran was outside.

"You know they say eavesdroppers never hear any good

of themselves," shouted Lois, and Dot grinned and got up to shut the door. "I can hear the kettle whistling, Mrs. Weedon," she whispered out into the hall.

Floss cleared her throat and asked if she could say something. Lois nodded, and Floss said she had been meaning to say it later, but last evening she had been walking back home when she saw a car coming at speed on the wrong side of the road. It was raining heavily and she couldn't see the number, but she thought it was a Land Rover 4x4. She turned off into Blackberry Gardens and so didn't see what happened, but she remembered thinking it was very dangerous if anyone was walking on the path. The spray was all over the place.

"Thanks, Floss. That could be important if we have to do any reporting to the police. I have been on the phone all morning before you all arrived. Now, if we could get back to New Brooms business, let's have client reports."

Dot said she would go last, so why didn't Floss go first, as she had a new client?

"Well, yes, I went with Mrs. M to meet Mrs. Prentise at Fletching. We had a good talk, and she gave us the impression that money was no object. It is a lovely house, and spotless, so should be a nice job for me."

"Sounds like a doddle! Does she have a family? No toys to trip over or nappy sacks left in a corner?"

"No, she's quite old. There's one room that I have to leave alone. Mrs. Prentise does it herself. It is a girl's room, all pink frills, and was her daughter's. Apparently, the daughter returns sometimes, so it's kept like a sort of shrine! A bit creepy, really."

"We'll learn more when Floss starts next Friday. As far as I am concerned, Mrs. Prentise looks like the perfect client!" Lois turned her papers over, and work progressed. Finally, it was time to end the meeting, and they all filed out with best wishes for Gran to recover.

Dot held back. "Can I have a private word, Mrs. M.?" she said.

"Shut the door, Dot. I have a little time before lunch."

"It's about Mrs. Weedon's escape from *them*."

"Dot? What on earth do you mean?"

"Like I was telling you. Opportunity arises, and they go to work."

"So it was likely to have been *them*? And Gran? Was she in the wrong place at the wrong time? Sounds a little like a bad movie, Dottie."

"Well, if you don't want to know, I'll go home right now." Dot stood up, full of huff.

"Don't be daft! Come on, tell me what's worrying you."

"It's that Mrs. Prentise, our new client. I know she's loaded, but her money was ill-gotten gains from her husband. He was a bit of a rival to my Handy in Tresham gangland. I'm not saying Floss will be in any danger or anything like that. It's just that you know what a lovely, sympathetic girl she is. I wouldn't want her to get too close to the old woman."

Lois sat down heavily in her chair. "Oh dear. Do you think we should send you instead?"

"She probably wouldn't accept me. We go back a long way, Diana Prentise and me. No, Floss will be fine, probably the ideal client, as you said. I'm sure you can give Floss a tactful warning. Maybe I shouldn't have brought it up. Sorry, Mrs. M."

Lois calmed her down, said that she was very glad to have such important information, and she would make sure Floss was warned before Friday, and then the girl would have the chance to back out, and Andrew could go in instead. "He would stand no nonsense. He's quite tough, though most people think that because he is an interior designer, he must be a bit, you know . . ."

Dot nodded. "Thanks for listening, Mrs. M. If I hear anything relating to Mrs. Weedon's nasty experience, I'll let you know."

"WHAT'S ALL THAT TALKING WITH DOT NIMMO?" GRAN WAS standing in front of the Rayburn, potatoes bubbling in a pan behind her, arms akimbo, frowning. "I bet you told her about me falling about!"

"Of course I told her, Mum. You know our Dot! If there's any chance of finding out who drove straight at you in the dark, then our Dot is the best source of help."

"Mm, well, if you say so. I don't want it spread all round the village, and you know what Dot Nimmo is."

"She lives in Tresham and doesn't go anywhere in Farnden, unless it's to a client."

"All round Tresham, then."

Lois gave up.

THIRTY-THREE

❧

OVER AT BRIGHAM, THE BAKEHOUSE WAS WARM FROM bread making all day. Aurora had been busy since four o'clock in the morning, and now, four o'clock in the afternoon, she made herself a cup of tea, made sure the bell from the shop was working and sat down in a comfortable chair with the newspaper. Milly had gone out, driving her mother's car to Farnden to collect up some shopping, and then going on into Tresham. Lois and Aurora had lately set up a reciprocal arrangement: Aurora selling her special hand-baked bread as a new line in Josie's shop and buying grocery basics in return.

Two minutes after opening the newspaper, Aurora's head drooped, and she fell into a light doze. She dreamed the old familiar dream, where Donald comes bounding up the steps into the house, kissing her affectionately on the cheek and pouring each of them a drink to tell her details of his selling trip. She felt the same stab of pleasure in having him home again, and, on waking to the shop bell's piercing sound, the old throb of pain. It was a dream, and he would never be coming home again, ever. Nor would she have sleepless hours of useless jealousy wondering whose arms he was in that night. She reminded herself of the pain he had caused her over the years, and tried to dismiss the whole thing from her mind.

Sighing deeply, she went through to the shop to see who had come in. She frowned. Nobody there? She went to the outer door and opened it. Stepping outside in case she could see someone leaving, she looked up and down the street and over at the main entrance to the Mill. Not a soul to be seen.

THIRTY-FOUR

THIS EVENING, AS SHE OFTEN DID, JOSIE CLOSED THE SHOP
and walked up to Meade House to check all was well
with her parents. And grandparent, of course. She found
them sitting round the kitchen table, studying the *Tresham
Evening News*.

"Hello, me duck. Come and sit down," said Derek.

"There's tea in the pot," said Gran. "Or I can make you
fresh?"

"Pot will do fine," said Josie and sat down next to Lois.
"What are you all studying so seriously?" she asked.

"Look at this!" said Gran, barely controlling her fury.

Josie looked. On the front page, a very good photo of
Gran appeared, occupying at least a quarter of the space.
Underneath, the headline said:

Ann Purser

Old Lady Target for Hit-and-Run!

"Oh dear," said Josie. "Who is responsible for this? From what you told me, it was just a little splash, and Gran tripped and fell. But not seriously!"

"Don't ask me!" said Gran. "Dot Nimmo! I don't intend to mention her ever again. She doesn't exist, and I shall be very glad if Lois will reconsider and give her her cards."

"Oh dear," repeated Josie. "But it's a lovely photo of you, Gran. Don't you think so, Dad? You look really glam!"

"For an old lady," said Gran, somewhat mollified. "But I still stand by what I say."

"So why don't I change the subject and tell you about my day in the shop?"

Lois looked gratefully at her daughter. "We could do with some nice news, love," she said.

"Well, Matthew went off on early duty, and so I opened up a little earlier than usual. The village is lovely at that time of day. Commuters not going through yet, and too early for the school run of four-by-fours, each with one child and its mother. Then the usual exciting shoppers buying a newspaper and a pack of sandwiches on their way to work in Tresham. My favourites come next."

"Dad and Mum and Gran?" Derek smiled fondly.

Josie shook her head. "Nope. The village's important population of retired ladies, emerging into the morning with their shopping bags and snippets of gossip. They congregate in the shop, make their purchases and have a talk among themselves. With cheery goodbyes to me, they leave. After that, I feel the best part of the day is over."

154

Gran sniffed. "You're just saying that to make me feel better," she said.

Josie shook her head. "No, I mean it, Gran. The older generation in our village mean a lot to me. I love to hear stories of the past, especially ones involving the shop. Maybe I'll write a book about it one day."

"Good girl," said Derek.

"Did Aurora bring the bread?" said Lois.

"Yes and no. The bread came, but Milly, her daughter, brought it and introduced herself. She's really nice. Stayed and had a chat until someone else came in. She's taking a year off to help her mother in the bakery. Then she goes back to nursing and a good job, she hopes. She's very pretty, isn't she, Mum? Not much like Donald to look at, except that dark hair."

"Let's hope that's the only resemblance," said Lois. "We can do without another nonswimmer!"

"Mum! I studiously avoided the subject. She must still be very cut up about it."

"Perhaps we should do a bit of matchmaking, and find her a husband. How about our Jamie? It's time he made up his mind."

"Oh no, I think she is very much the career girl. Still, look at me! Excellent results in A-levels, and ended up behind a shop counter . . ."

"I think shop owner, wife and maybe soon, we hope, mother, is a very busy career for anyone," said Gran.

"It's not my shop. It's Mum and Dad's, and I just work there." Josie frowned, and Lois looked meaningfully at Derek.

"We might as well tell you now," said Derek. "We intend to hand over the shop entirely to you, as soon as we've seen the lawyers. Partly because of inheritance tax, but mainly because you deserve to make it your own. Is that okay?"

Josie rushed over and kissed them both, and said she was a horrid ungrateful daughter, but meant to make amends by opening a string of supergrocers named Meade's Markets.

"Must go now," she added, "and do my bit as housewife and cook. See you tomorrow, Gran? Will you be down for your chockies?"

After she had left, they looked at each other. "That's done, then," said Lois. "I think we can safely say she was pleased! Now, Mum, have you calmed down enough to read beyond the headline? I think you'll find you come out as 'Feisty Gran Fights Off Muggers.'"

"Nice that she's met Aurora's daughter," said Gran, ignoring Lois. "They could get to be good friends. Maybe Jamie will be back soon, and we can introduce them."

Thirty-Five

M ILLY BLACK'S EARS WERE NOT BURNING AS THE MEADES discussed her. She was too worried about her mother, who seemed nervous and unable to settle.

The evening had dragged by, with Aurora clearly not wanting to talk. At nine o'clock, she said she thought she would have an early night. She had asked Milly to make sure to turn off the telly and gone up to bed, hoping for no bad dreams.

All to be expected in bereavement, thought Milly. She had studied the subject, but now that it was her own mother, it was different. She herself had not dreamed about her father since his death. Maybe that was the more unusual reaction.

She turned off the late news, which was full of doom and gloom as usual, and directed her thoughts towards nice Josie Vickers in the shop. A good friend, perhaps, for her year working for Mum in the bakery.

Thirty-Six

❧

Next morning, Aurora felt anxious, on edge, and when Milly came back and was able to take over, she went out of the shop door into the sunshine. Three old men sat on the millpond wall, throwing food for the ducks.

The men came from the White House, a nice old Victorian mansion at the top of the hill. It had been a small school, but now gave shelter and care for men who mostly had lived up to then on the streets. Now they were clean and relatively happy, though some talked wistfully of their nomadic lives. Occasionally, Aurora would join them on the wall and listen to their colourful life stories.

"Are you okay, Mum?" Milly looked closely at her mother. She was very pale this morning, and her hands were shaking as she handed Milly a mug of coffee.

"Fine, thanks," Aurora said. "Will you be around this afternoon? I need to go out around half past one, but should be back by three. Would that be all right with you?"

"Yeah, o'course," Milly said. "Going anywhere exciting?"

Aurora frowned. "I wouldn't call an appointment with the dentist exciting, but you never know . . ." She smiled, and Milly felt relieved.

Lois was busy in her office when the phone rang. It was Douglas, calling from home. "I'm off sick for a few days," he said. "Fluey cold, so don't come visiting. Susie and the kids are all fine at the moment, so I am quarantined in the back bedroom! Just thought I'd give you a ring to see if there's been any progress in finding the hit-and-run merchant."

"You poor chap! Sorry to hear you're poorly. Not like you to stay in bed!" Lois's eldest had always been the tough one, along with his dad. She thought of rushing over to make sure he was being looked after properly, then laughed at herself for being so foolish.

"No, no news," she answered. "Everything seems to have gone quiet. Calm before the storm, maybe. Still, we don't want any more drama from that quarter. Maybe the late Donald Black is back under suspicion. He had an alibi, of course, but it might not be so watertight as he had said."

"Yes, and are they still thinking he could have fallen in and drowned, and been carried along by the wheel, and so not been murdered by anybody, including himself?"

"I think it is still a possibility. I keep forgetting to ask

Aurora if he could swim, but even if he could, the current could have been strong and taken him to the wheel before he could swim away."

"Complicated, isn't it? Still, old Cowgill will get to the bottom of it. With your help, of course."

"That's quite enough of that, young man! Now you be good and do what Susie tells you."

"Ah, here she comes, Florence Nightingale, bearing steaming coffee and a jam doughnut. Bye, Mum; keep in touch."

It certainly was complicated, thought Lois, as she tried to concentrate on her New Brooms tasks. She meant to call Floss in for a chat about Mrs. Prentise and her dodgy family. If Dot thought it would be quite safe, then there was nothing to worry about. And she would soon let her know if there was any reason for withdrawing Floss. She picked up the phone and dialled Floss's mobile.

"Hi, Floss. Nothing serious, but could you drop in at lunchtime? Something to tell you, but nothing to worry about. See you then."

By the time Floss rang the doorbell, Gran had been down to the shop to buy up any unsold copies of last evening's newspaper, saying that the fewer people who saw it the better. Lois suspected that she was in fact cutting out the photo and the story, and sending it off to far-flung friends.

"And quite right, too," she said to Derek at lunchtime, while Gran was upstairs. "She *was* a brave lady, and deserves a pat on the back."

"What's on your diary for this afternoon, me duck? I

have to go over to Brigham to do a job, and thought I'd look in on Aurora. She needs all the support she can get."

"And Milly, too," said Lois. "Give them my love and say I'll be over very soon. What time do you think you'll be finished?"

"Around five, I should think. I'll call at the bakery on my way home."

The doorbell rang, and Gran rushed to answer it. It was Floss, and Lois took her into the office.

"This won't take long, Flossie," she said. "Sit down, my dear. Would you like a coffee? No? Right, well, I'll come straight to the point. It is about Mrs. Prentise. Our new client, and the one neither of us liked very much. Well, Dot Nimmo has told me that her family were part of a semicriminal organisation in Tresham in the past. It has all fallen apart now, apparently, and good policing has put them out of business, except for easy, random criminal acts like mugging. But I thought I should tell you, in case you didn't fancy it. What do you think?"

Floss shrugged. "Doesn't bother me, Mrs. M. I can always defend meself with me mop and bucket. No, but seriously, thanks for telling me. It might be useful, in fact, for me to keep my ear to the ground. Useful for you, I mean."

Lois smiled. "Thanks, Floss. Now, I won't keep you. You're at Brigham this afternoon, aren't you? Derek's over there later, but you might look in at the bakery and say hello."

The afternoon went quickly for Lois. She had a chat with Cowgill on the phone, and was irritated by his insistence that they were no further forward in their investigations.

"Are you being straight with me?" she said.

"Would I be anything else?" he said.

"Yes, if it was necessary," she answered. "And before I forget, was Donald Black a strong swimmer?"

There was a moment's silence, and then he said that he did not know what constituted a strong swimmer, but his wife had said he certainly could swim. As far as she knew, he had not been swimming for years, as he hated getting his hair wet.

"Oh Lor, what a Charlie! Poor old Aurora. Fancy being married to that! Anyway, thanks for the info. Please keep me in touch!"

THIRTY-SEVEN

⁓

AROUND SIX O'CLOCK, LOIS WAS BEGINNING TO WONDER when Derek would be back. Of course, he might have been held up chatting to Aurora and Milly, and that was a good thing. Poor things must be glad of a sensible man to lift their spirits.

The phone rang, and this time it was Derek.

"Lois? Something funny going on here. Aurora went out about one thirty saying she'd be back at three, and Milly has heard nothing since. Poor kid is a bit worried, naturally enough. She is sure something has happened, as her mother would never not let her know if she was going to be this late. You haven't heard anything, I suppose? Aurora said she was going to the dentist, but Milly phoned him, and he said he hadn't seen her. She had an appointment, apparently, but she didn't show up and he had heard nothing."

"Odd. But tell Milly not to worry. If she hears nothing by sevenish, I'll call Matthew and see what he thinks we should do. Can you stay there with her? I expect she's in a frail state anyway. Good. I'll wait to hear from you. Meanwhile, I'll ring Floss. She was going to call in at the bakery this afternoon to say hello. She might give us a clue. Bye."

UNABLE TO RELAX, LOIS GAVE GRAN A BRIEF ACCOUNT OF WHAT had happened, and they sat staring at the telly, but not listening to a word. Lois looked at her watch.

"There's news, Mum, on the other channel." She flicked over, and they listened carefully this time, but there was no mention of missing persons.

"Of course not," said Gran. "I don't know why you are all making such a fuss. The woman has probably gone shopping somewhere else, or met a friend and gone back with her to supper. There's dozens of reasons why she hasn't come home when expected."

Then the phone rang again, and it was Derek.

"No Aurora, I'm afraid, so Milly says I should come home. She'll be perfectly all right, she says."

"I should think so, too," said Gran sniffily.

Milly had cheered up after assuring Derek she would be all right. She even said she could not think her mother was in real danger.

"She has no enemies," she insisted to Derek. "Everybody

loves her, and she is doing so well in the shop because people like to come in and have a cosy chat in the warmth of the bakery. Not a soul has ever said a word against her. My dad used to say that. He always said she would go straight to heaven one day, with no stopping on the way."

THIRTY-EIGHT

❧

Next morning, Milly had heard nothing from her mother, and so put up a notice in the bakery window, saying it would be shut until further notice, then returned to the bakehouse to turn off the oven. Then she had a thought. Maybe if she kept the shop open, selling what bread there was left from yesterday, and muffins still in date, then she could engage customers in conversation and maybe get some clues as to her mother's whereabouts.

She took down the notice and unlocked the shop door. Mum always wore a fresh apron and handled all bread with thin plastic gloves. She prepared herself for her first customer, and was pleased to see Floss, a little early for her day to clean the bakehouse and living quarters.

"Morning, Milly. Sorry I couldn't call in last evening,

but had to work late. How are you doing? I can stay a bit longer this morning if that would be a help."

"Shall we start with a coffee? That would be much more helpful than a clean floor. I am now really worried about Mum, Floss. Why doesn't she get in touch? Do you think she's held somewhere and not allowed to? Oh Lord, I just don't understand it."

Floss calmly made the coffee, and sat down on a bench beside Milly. "Let's talk about something else for a bit," she said. "Would you like to hear about my new client? I know Mrs. M doesn't like us to discuss our other ladies—or gents—but we'll make an exception. You probably know the woman. Mrs. Prentise, over at Fletching. Lives in the lap of luxury, surrounded by the ill-gotten gains of her late husband's criminal activities." She laughed. "That's strictly between us, of course."

"Prentise, did you say? I think she's one of Mum's bread customers."

"Nothing but the best for Mrs. Prentise," said Floss. "She's just bought two new cars. A Jaguar for showing off, and a scarlet Fiat 500 for popping over to see friends. Funny woman. One minute she's warm and friendly, and the next clams up like an oyster and goes all chilly. Still, I suppose I'll get used to her. As Mrs. M says, we don't have to like our clients, just do a good job."

Milly managed a smile. "I've got her now. Once or twice when I've been home, she's come in with her daughter. A really tarty-looking female, Gloria, of course, with a lot to say for herself. Between you and me, I reckon she was after my dad. Several times, he came through the shop while they were here, and she was all over him."

That must have been jolly for Aurora, thought Floss. But she said no more about the Prentises, and after cautioning Milly to forget immediately all she had reported, otherwise she'd be getting her cards from Mrs. M, she started off upstairs to begin cleaning.

Milly's next customer was Lois. "I'm not checking up on Floss," she said, smiling warmly. She was pleased that Milly looked much more relaxed. Floss working her magic, she thought. "I just wanted to call and see how you are, dear," she said. "Josie said you had a good night, with the aid of a pill. Still, however, it will have done you good. It's really great to see you've opened up."

"I thought I might chat up one or two customers and see if they have any news of Mum."

"I'm sure you'll be hearing from her very soon," Lois said. "It could be that the dreadful thing that happened to your father has knocked her sideways for a bit. Does happen, I believe. She's probably not thinking straight. But she'll be her old self any time now. And think how pleased she'll be to see you're keeping the bakery going!"

"I can't bake bread, though. I'll be open until all the other stock is sold, anyway. And by then, perhaps we'll know . . ." Her lip quivered, and she sniffed.

"I'll have two small wholemeal loaves, please!" said Lois breezily. "And Josie said she'll bring supper when and if she comes along tonight. You won't be alone, Milly, and we're all doing our very best to help."

"I am really grateful," said Milly, close to tears again.

"You'd think with my nurse training I'd be used to bad news, but when it's your own mother . . ."

"Chin up, love. By this evening, we're bound to have some news on police progress. Not to mention a little ferretin' on my part! See you later."

It was not until later that Lois remembered Milly tearfully missing her mother, but with no mention of her father, except that Gloria Prentise had been more than friendly with him. A chat with Gloria might be productive. She drove home whistling loudly, and Jemima, curled up in the back, twitched. If dogs could frown, she would have frowned her displeasure.

INSTEAD OF DRIVING STRAIGHT HOME, LOIS DECIDED TO GO INTO Tresham and call on Dot Nimmo. Dot was her source of useful information on the underworld of town, and would certainly be able to tell her where to find Gloria. Mrs. Prentise had given her the impression that she was seldom at home in Fletching and her frilly bedroom was almost never used.

Dot would be at home this morning, and Lois drew up outside her house, making a mental note to call in later at New Brooms office, at the other end of the street.

"Gloria Prentise? What on earth do you want to see that scrubber for?" Dot was not one for mincing her words, and Lois laughed.

"I need to talk to her about Donald Black. To call a spade a spade, you obviously know she is almost certainly a high-class prostitute. Her family is loaded, and she doesn't need to do it. Like a lot of rich kids, she likes the danger and spice involved, I suppose. Don't forget she was Sylvia Fountain's cousin."

"As if!" said Dot firmly. "And don't go mixing yourself up with that lot! I can tell you all you need to know."

"Thanks, Dottie. But I would just like to meet Glorious Gloria. Do you know where I might track her down?"

Dot looked at her watch. "The Purple Dog," she said. "Next to St. Cuthbert's, in Market Street. She's there most lunchtimes, picking up messages. Know what I mean? But you have to take care, Mrs. M. Take my advice and stay away."

"I'm sure you are right, Dot, and I will be careful. But Aurora is a good friend of mine, and I am very fond of her daughter, who as good as told me that Gloria was one of her father's girlfriends. Anything I can do to help at the moment . . ."

"Mm, well, have it your way. But watch your back. What about old Cowgill? Isn't he on the case? He's pretty good at finding lost dogs, so he might even produce Aurora Black very soon."

THIRTY-NINE

⁓

THE PURPLE DOG WAS AN UNGLAMOROUS NIGHTCLUB IN the backstreets of Tresham. Purple paint peeled off an unlikely looking poodle, mounted on a sign that squeaked rustily in the wind. Lois parked her van outside the front door, where she could keep it in sight. Locked vehicles were child's play for the villains of Market Street.

When she walked into the bar, she knew immediately which of the drinkers was Gloria Prentise. Her mop of red hair shone like a good deed in a naughty world. Not that the Purple Dog was all that naughty. It had had its teeth drawn by the police some time ago. That hair! thought Lois. One hundred percent natural, she was sure. She remembered how beautifully she had shown off the jewellery when she came to the party with her mother. Gloria the model and Gloria the comforter of lonely men. Unfortunately, today her face did not match the beauty. Heavily made up, with a falsely bright smile, she was deep in conversation with a very fat man, who overflowed the bar stool on which he perched like an overweight pigeon.

"This is a private club, missus. Members only," said the man, frowning at Lois.

"I am a visitor only, looking for Gloria Prentise."

"That's me," said Gloria. "As I suspect you already know. And don't worry about her," she added, speaking to the man on the stool. "Cowgill's bit of stuff."

"I'll ignore that," said Lois pleasantly. "I wonder if you could spare me a few moments. I am trying to find out what has happened to a friend of mine—"

"—Aurora Black?" said Gloria. "She's okay, as far as I know. Something happened to her, has it? I expect she's mourning her dear husband. What a crumb! If you ask me, he got what was coming to him."

Lois's eyebrows shot up. "And what was that?"

"Don't come the innocent with me, Mrs. Cleverdick Meade! He met a watery end, stupid sod. Probably couldn't swim. And that wasn't the only thing he couldn't do. Not with goody-goody Aurora, anyway. Take my advice and forget all about the Brigham Blacks." She downed half a glass of red wine and turned away.

The fat man slid off his stool and moved towards Lois. "Are you going to clear off, or shall I throw you out?" he said. "And don't even think of becoming a member."

Lois laughed in his face. "Whatever makes you think I would ever want to join your rotten club?" she said, and walked smartly out and into the street. A huddle of young kids stood at the corner, staring as she drove off in her van. Her heart was thudding, and she took some deep breaths. Derek would be furious if he knew she had been frightened by the Purple Dog.

HAZEL WAS COMFORTINGLY CALM AND CONFIDENT, LOOKING UP brightly from her desk as Lois walked in.

"Hi, Mrs. M! I wasn't expecting you, was I?"

"No, spur of the moment, Hazel. How are you and your family?"

A short and entertaining account of Hazel's farming husband and her small daughter's narrow escape from a rampant cockerel was just what Lois needed, and she accepted an offer of coffee and chat gracefully.

It was really stupid, she told herself as Hazel disappeared into the kitchen. There was nothing seriously threatening about Gloria or her friend. They were unpleasant, certainly, but not much more. If they did know the whereabouts of Aurora, they were not telling, and she would have to think of some other way of finding out at least the likelihood of her being abducted and held somewhere local.

But why? What possible gain could anyone possibly expect from Aurora Black, who had never caused anyone harm, and, it now seemed, had had quite a lot to put up with from husband Donald? If it was money, it was a waste of time. Aurora had often said they had sacrificed all their spare cash on giving Milly a good education and training for her chosen profession. Then it must be something else. Her silence? She must have known all about Sylvia and Gloria being mistresses of Donald, and decided to let it happen a good while ago.

Then Lois remembered one occasion when she had been talking to Aurora on the phone, and Donald had interrupted, ranting on at Aurora. But he had apologised, and they had seemed as easy as ever with each other afterwards.

Was it possible that Aurora had *not* known about Donald's affairs? After all, he was away overnight around the country, and unless she had actually made attempts to find out about his secret life, he could easily have had a clear field. But the local ones? Jewellery parties. The ideal opportunity to make assignations, et cetera, et cetera . . .

"I don't know, Hazel," she said, as the coffee was put down in front of her. "There seems to be no end to the number of people determined to mess up their own perfectly good lives."

"Not me, I hope!" said Hazel. "We've recently had a litter of ten little piglets. Now who could want more than that?"

"The butcher, I suppose," said Lois, laughing. "Any news for me, new clients, customer complaints, shortage of dusters?"

Hazel said there were two new clients for Lois to visit, no complaints and no shortage of anything except beeswax polish.

They chatted on, until Lois felt completely relaxed and stood up from her chair to turn to the door. A figure stood outside, blocking her way out. It was a woman, and there was no mistaking the head of fiery curls.

"Ah, just the person I wanted to see," said Gloria. "I thought I might find you here. Now then," she continued, walking forward to face Lois. "You said you wanted a few minutes of my time, and that fool turned you out. So now here I am. What did you want? No, don't say anything. It was about Aurora Black, wasn't it? How long have you got? We shall need to sit down. Half an hour should do it. You're Hazel Thornbull, aren't you? Well, you can take a break. Have a walk round the shops, but be back in an hour's time. I have work to do."

For once, Lois was speechless. She nodded at Hazel, sat down and waited for Gloria to continue.

FORTY

꒓

"Fɪʀsᴛ ᴏғ ᴀʟʟ," sᴀɪᴅ Gʟᴏʀɪᴀ, "I ᴋɴᴏᴡ ʏᴏᴜ ᴛʜɪɴᴋ ᴛʜᴇ worst of Donald Black, and it's true he wasn't much good. But he wasn't very bad, either. I first met him at the Purple Dog. He was as drunk as a lord, and they were about to throw him out. I took him up to my flat and sobered him up. And that's all, I swear. I knew he was my cousin Sylvia's lover, and she was fond of him in a small way. I don't expect you to believe me, nor do I care whether you believe me or not, but we work for the club, encouraging customers. There's plenty of unhappy men who like a drink and a chat with a woman who'll give them a smile, but nothing else. No complications."

"And now there's only you, Gloria," said Lois, finding her voice. "I remember you from the jewellery party. Weren't you modelling the stuff? Which leads me to ask, wouldn't

you call being strangled with a necklace a complication?"
The last thing she had expected was Gloria turning out to
be a warmhearted friend to all!

Gloria frowned. "That was below the belt, Mrs. Meade.
Sylvia and I were cousins. More like sisters for years. I'll catch
the wicked sod who killed her if it's the last thing I do, and if
what I've heard is true, you are the best person to help me."

"I am not so sure about that," said Lois. "Why don't you
leave it to the police? Cowgill's pretty good at his job. Could
be the safest option."

"I told you. You have the ear of Inspector Cowgill. That's
well known in my circles. He would certainly not cooperate
with me, but with you, yes, and I could contribute to you
what I know about our side of it. Sylvia was family, but more
than that. Like I said, she was both sister and best friend
to me."

"But don't you accept that Donald Black must have killed
her? Perhaps because she was threatening to tell Aurora?
Something like that?"

Gloria's angry red face clashed with her quivering curls.
"What's the matter with you, Lois Meade? My Sylvia would
never have done that. Anyway, she had no need. He kept her
wanting nothing, never short of cash. And I know she was
fond of the useless idiot. We told each other everything, and
she told me he used to say he was leaving everything he
owned to her in his will."

"So, if it wasn't some other punter, who? Somebody who
wanted more than a smile and a friendly chat? And why that
necklace? It was a particularly nasty murder weapon."

Gloria stared at her. "For God's sake, woman, isn't it

obvious? She had Donald Black's promotion pack with her, and was due to be at a party next day somewhere up north. The necklace was handy."

"Have you told Cowgill this? No, silly question. How about this: why haven't you told Cowgill about this?"

"You can answer that one yourself. I got to go, anyway. The thing I want you to know is this. We're on the same side. I didn't kill Donald Black, nor did he kill Sylvia. He couldn't kill a wasp! Who does that leave? Person or persons unknown? Think on, Mrs. Meade. I've been thinking it would be very useful to get details of the postmortem. One for you to take on. And, since there may have been money involved, a look at Donald Black's last will and testament would be extremely helpful, don't you think? I could maybe arrange to be there when it is read."

"So, do we have a deal?" said Lois. "We must work together on finding who killed Sylvia and Donald? If you know anything I should know, you know where to find me. And vice versa."

Gloria stood up and marched to the door. "We'll find him or her, rest assured. And if Aurora Black turns up, let me know. Please."

FORTY-ONE

꒰

B Y SUPPER TIME, LOIS HAD DECIDED SHE WOULD TELL DEREK the whole story of her meeting with Gloria Prentise. She knew that sooner or later she would have to report to Cowgill, but if she intended to take Gloria up on her declaration that they were on the same side, and therefore it followed that they would work together, this was going to be a big risk. The Prentises were trouble. At least, they had been, in the past. Was it likely they had all become reformed characters? No, it was not. But, then again, Gloria would have an ear to sources of information that might help in finding Aurora. That was her chief concern. The deaths of Sylvia and Donald should take second place. If they were linked, so much the better. But for Milly's sake alone, she needed to find Aurora as soon as possible.

"Penny for your thoughts, love," said Derek. Gran had

gone up to her bedroom to watch television, and Lois and Derek sat on, looking at the sporting pages of the newspaper.

"Oh, I was miles away," said Lois.

"In Tresham? Fletching? Waltonby, Brigham? A certain bakery opposite the Mill House Hotel?"

Lois nodded. "Yep. Aurora and Milly. And something else. I had a visitor when I was talking to Hazel in our Tresham office today. She followed me down from the Purple Dog. Gloria Prentise, it was."

"Who? Prentise, did you say? One of that lot?"

"Yes, Gloria Prentise. Daughter of Mrs. Diana Prentise, our new client in Fletching. Gloria was a cousin of Sylvia Fountain, the woman found strangled in the Mill House Hotel. Gloria and Sylvia both worked at the Purple Dog in town. No, don't laugh, Derek! It's serious."

"I'll say it is! Did she want a job with you? I can't see her on her knees with a scrubbing brush. Though scrubber is not a bad description, if I'm thinking of the right one. Tarty redhead?"

"Yes. She said we were both on the same side, that she did not kill Donald Black, nor did he kill her precious cousin Sylvia. She means to discover who did, though she is not much concerned with Donald. Her cousin was like a sister to her, and she intends to find out who strangled her with a Brigham Luxury Jewellery pearl necklace. God knows what she'll do if she finds the culprit."

"And when you say you are both on the same side, I hope you don't mean you are having anything to do with it?"

"Only so far as it touches Aurora and Milly. I must try to

help them, Derek. Else I'm a rotten friend, and you know me better than that."

Derek sighed. "Well, thanks for telling me. At least I know now what is going on. Have you told Cowgill?"

"No. What do you think?"

"Tell him. The Prentise woman will expect you to, so no harm done there. You'd do well to have no further contact with her, unless she approaches you. And then make sure you're in a public place."

"Derek! Aren't you being a bit overdramatic? She's no reason to do me harm . . . Oh dear, I see what you mean. Aurora Black has disappeared without a trace. Okay, I'll remember."

"Come on, me duck. Let's forget all about it and go upstairs for a cuddle."

"What about the washing up?"

"I'll stack the dishes while you go upstairs and warm the bed."

ALONE IN HER BEDROOM IN THE BRIGHAM BAKERY, MILLY BLACK sat hunched up in bed, a woolly shawl around her shoulders, reading Jane Austen. The affair of Elizabeth Bennet and Mr. Darcy was the only thing that could take her mind off her vanished mother, and she was deep into the goings-on at Longbourn when she heard a sound coming from downstairs.

She froze. Then she closed the book and swung her legs out of bed. In bare feet, she tiptoed downstairs, collecting a golf club from the umbrella stand as she went.

Room by room, her heart thudding hard, she looked all round, leaving the kitchen until last. If there was someone there, she could always make a run for it out of the door.

"Hullo? Is anyone there?" she called in a tremulous voice.

No answer. Everywhere was quiet and still. Finally, she decided the sound must have come from the hotel opposite, and she climbed back into bed. As she drifted slowly into sleep, she remembered she had left an unwashed coffee mug on the draining board. Mum would have been cross about that, she told herself. Always start the day with a clean slate. That's what she taught her from an early age. "If only you were here to tell me now," Milly said softly and sadly.

First thing next morning, Milly went down to let out the cat and open up. She was hoping to have a go at making bread dough and then a trial batch of wholemeal loaves. She would not be able to sell them, even if they were perfect, because she was unsure about health and safely rules on selling fresh produce. She guessed that if she gave the loaves away, as a trial baking, there would be no problem. Provided that the loaves were edible!

She grabbed a stale bun, spread jam on it thickly, and downed it with a glass of milk. That would do for breakfast. Then a quick shower, and she was ready to begin. A fresh apron and the protective gloves, and she measured out the flour and salt in large pans to warm in the oven. And, of course, to switch on the oven!

It warmed up quickly, and Milly went to the sink to rinse

her glass and plate. There would be room enough in the dish-washer for last night's coffee mug. But it was not there.

"Must have put it in after all," she muttered. "At least that was one thing I did right yesterday."

A knock on the locked shop door took her attention, and she went to take in the morning newspaper. Spreading it out on the table, she leafed through for anything new about her missing mother. Same old report, whittled down. But the police said on a different page that as a result of a number of useful reports, they were following up several leads and expected to find Aurora soon. Well, she had been away for only two nights, and Milly consoled herself with the thought that there was another whole day ahead when she might come back.

FORTY-TWO

⤲

LOIS HAD STARTED THE DAY OPTIMISTICALLY, HAVING A peaceful conversation with Gran about weekend shopping and final preparations for the jewellery party. As she made phone calls necessary to the smooth working of New Brooms, she was determined to put Gloria Prentise out of her mind for the moment. She had not forgotten that she had more or less promised to find out the results of the Fountain postmortem, but she had other things to think about. She hoped that Gloria would have the sense to do the same. Almost the last thing she had said was that Donald's will would be read shortly, and she had ways of finding out what was in it. She would let Lois know, she said, if it contained anything of interest.

"Meanwhile, there is the jewellery party to think about,

you and Joan, to take place tomorrow. Dot Nimmo was asking about it."

"It's time that Nimmo woman learned to mind her own business! She sticks her nose in everywhere, and it's time you got rid of her."

"That's my business, Mum," said Lois. "Dot is a very useful member of the New Brooms team. Anyway, she'd heard that this party was to be one of several. Is that true?"

"Yes, it is. But it is not the first of any particular number. It might be a one and only, depending on how it goes. If we have any stuff left over, we shall donate it to the hospice shop."

"And where is this party to be held?"

"In the village reading room."

"This village?"

"Of course. And if you've finished with the Spanish inquisition, I'll go and get on. I'm putting notices around the village. We don't want huge crowds. It's just a fun thing for me and Joan to do."

"Right," said Lois. "I presume you won't turn down an offer of help. I'm free on Saturday, all day."

Gran sniffed. "Naturally, we shall welcome any offers of help. Josie has already said she'd come down after the shop shuts. We shall open to the public from two o'clock in the afternoon until six o'clock in the evening."

"Why didn't you tell me about this earlier, Mum?"

"Because you would have tried to stop us. Too late now, so you'd better come with good grace and help us have an enjoyable afternoon."

Ann Purser

*　　*　　*

FEELING A LITTLE CHASTENED, LOIS DECIDED TO WALK DOWN TO
Stone House, and have a chat with her sometime assistant,
Mrs. Tollervey-Jones. It was just possible she might have
heard something about Aurora from her friends in high
places. The old lady had been an active magistrate in her
time and still had a keen interest in any ferretin' that Lois
might be involved in.

"Good morning!" said a firm voice from the garden at the
front of the house. "Just having an argument with a thorny
rose. But I'm winning, and shall be with you in two ticks."

"Here, let me help," said Lois, struggling to hold back
a stem with brutal thorns. "There you are, all free and
unwounded. I wonder if you are able to spare me a couple of
minutes for a small chat?"

"With pleasure, my dear," said Mrs. T-J, straightening
her tangled hair. "Come on indoors. A small sloe gin might
be a good idea. What do you think?"

The house was calm and cool, and Lois felt immediately more relaxed. After chatting about village matters
for a while, she brought up the subject of Aurora's disappearance.

"I am trying very hard to help find what has happened
to her. She is a good friend, and I am fond of her daughter,
who is trying to carry on the bakery by herself. It is so
unlike Aurora to have done such a thing deliberately, without letting Milly know, and I reckon she is lost somewhere
with her memory knocked sideways by Donald's death."

"Great Scott!" Mrs. T-J opened her eyes wide. "That nice

woman who has the bakery at Brigham? I heard something about it, but thought she must have turned up by now."

"No, I am afraid not. I wondered if you have any idea how we might find her?"

"Dogs," said Mrs. T-J, without turning a hair.

"I beg your pardon?" said Lois.

"Dogs. Sniffer dogs. Excellent for finding missing people and things."

Lois stared at her. Had she flipped her lid, the dear old thing?

"I am quite serious, Lois. If her daughter has something with her mother's scent on it, we can make a start at once. No time to lose, before the scent grows cold."

"When do you suggest?"

"This afternoon. Pick me up around two o'clock. Ring up the daughter and get her to sort out some nice smelly things."

"And the dog? My Jemima would be useless. And anyway, surely the police will have done all that?"

"The dog I am talking about has beaten every dog in the county at finding and fetching. And even if the police have been there, it won't hurt to make sure. No, let us give it a try. If no luck, then there will be no harm done. And Milly will be reassured that something is still being done to find her mother. Oh yes, I have a friend who has just the animal we need. I'll have him here by two. Now, off you go, my dear. We have work to do."

FORTY-THREE

✑

WHEN LOIS, MRS. T-J AND DOG HENRY ARRIVED IN Brigham, they could see at once that Milly had the shop door open and was standing at the entrance.

"I'll take Henry to lift his leg in the meadow for ten minutes," said Mrs. T-J, "while you prepare the girl and smooth the way for what may be a fruitless exercise. But worth trying!"

As Lois watched the pair walking over past the mill-pond and into the meadow, she remembered the awful day when she and Aurora had walked so cheerfully, looking forward to their drink in the hotel and Jemima enjoying chasing pigeons into flight from the low brick wall surrounding the entrance to the bar. And then the waterwheel and its sad burden appearing in front of them in the restaurant. She shook herself, and walked to where Milly stood, waving.

"Hi, Milly! Glad to see you're still open."

"Nice to see you, Mrs. Meade. Come on in and have the one free loaf left."

"Free? Are you sure? Is it stale bread?"

"No, I made it myself as a trial, and it has turned out really well. I cut one loaf in half to make sure, and it is fine. Here, let me wrap it for you, and then we'll go and have a coffee. I can't say customers are exactly queuing up. 'Missing Mother' story has gone cold, I suppose. Do you have any news? Inspector Cowgill checked in here this morning, but he didn't have anything new to say. Officially confident, though."

Lois shook her head and said she would love a coffee, but she was on a Tollervey-Jones errand, and had to get back more or less straightaway.

"As I said on the phone, we are to go on a Sherlock Holmes–type hunt, bearing some intimate garment of Aurora's, and accompanied by a sniffer dog. She seems very confident, and sometimes she is right. So do you mind?"

"Of course not! Why didn't we think of that?" She smiled a wobbly smile, and disappeared upstairs.

When Mrs. T-J returned, she instructed Milly to go off somewhere within reach. "Why not go and call on a friend? Come back in an hour or so, and don't worry; we shan't disturb your mother's personal things. Off you go now."

Milly set off reluctantly, leaving the two standing in the shop. When she was out of sight, they began work. Lois was full of admiration with the way Mrs. T-J seemed to know exactly how to handle Henry. Nose to the ground after a good sniff, he went from place to place, tail wagging. Then out of the bedroom and downstairs, picking up scents all the way. Finally they ended up in the shop, and Mrs. T-J said nothing unexpected had happened. Naturally, scents of Aurora were everywhere. Then she opened the door, and led Henry out into the road.

He immediately turned around and headed back into the shop.

"No, no lad, come along, this way. We'll go over to Aurora's car. Come along, this way, Henry!"

Henry refused to move. He sat down by the shop door, a mutinous expression on his face.

"Now what?" said Lois. "Why won't he follow her scent to the car, or to anywhere else outside? She must have gone somewhere."

"Unless she was lifted up and carried. Don't mention that to Milly, but it begins to look like the most likely explanation. I'll let Henry off the lead and see where he takes us."

The dog pottered about the shop for a few minutes, sniffing in all corners, then he returned to the bakehouse and sat down by the oven.

"For heaven's sake!" said Lois. "He's found himself a nice warm billet and given up. Look at his face! He looks very pleased with himself. I think that's it, isn't? We'd better get him back in my van and wait for Milly to come home."

"He'll do no harm there, Lois. Let him stay. We'll keep an eye on him."

They sat chatting for a while, until they heard the shop-door bell, and Lois went to see who was there. It was Milly back again, and she was told that Henry had failed. She nodded. "I thought so," she said. "I can't see how he could pick up a single scent from all the others around since Mum went missing. Never mind, it was worth a try. Where is he now?"

In the bakehouse, Henry was still sitting in guarding mode beside the oven, and when Milly approached to give him a stroke, he growled at her, baring his teeth with his ears back.

"Henry!" said Mrs. T-J. "This is Milly, a friend. Come along; we'll put him in the van and be on our way. Thank you, dear, for being so accommodating. We shall keep in touch, eh, Lois? Goodbye now."

"WASN'T THAT RATHER ODD?" SAID LOIS, AS THEY DROVE BACK to Farnden. "I mean, Henry had picked up the scent so obviously going in all the places where Aurora would have been."

Mrs. T-J glanced into the back of the van, where Henry had dozed off, unaware that he had been a disappointment. He had an old gardening glove of Aurora's, the only thing that would get him into Lois's van.

"Where did Milly get that glove from?" Mrs. T-J asked Lois.

"From a pair on a high shelf in the kitchen. He does seem specially attached to it. Perhaps we should have given Henry more time?"

"Not sure, Lois," Mrs. T-J said. "I suppose it is possible there were too many traces. But it is odd that he wouldn't budge from the bakehouse. We must think some more. Now, if you could drop me outside the shop, I must pick up a few odds and ends from Josie. I'll take Henry, and return him to his owner. She may have other suggestions."

FORTY-FOUR

❧

Back home in Farnden, Lois had offered to take Gran and Joan into town in the van to collect the jewellery for the party, but admitted that the single extra seat in the back was very uncomfortable, and so she agreed to go with Gran in Joan's car. Joan was a careful driver, and although Lois longed to put her foot on the accelerator on long stretches of dual carriageway, she settled in the back of the Rover and thought about Aurora.

Milly had been so disappointed that Henry had given them no pointers to the direction Aurora might have gone. But remembering the big oven where he sat down on guard, something was wrong there, thought Lois, as they cruised at thirty miles an hour along the empty road leading into Tresham.

"Now, Joan, it's first left after the lights. Or is it right? No, it's second on the left and then sharp right," said Gran.

Lois cleared her throat. "Don't think so, Mum. It's next left; then halfway down is the jeweller's shop. You can't miss it. It's got a large old clock hanging outside."

"That's what I said," protested Gran.

Fortunately, Joan knew exactly where it was, and pulled up smoothly under the clock. "Here we are, then, Elsie. Out you get."

"Is it safe to leave the car out here?" said Gran.

"Oh yes. Mr. Trinder has everything alarmed, being as it is a jeweller's," said Lois.

The three were welcomed in, and invited into a room at the back of the shop, where the jewellery ordered had been laid out for inspection on a large dining table covered with green baize.

"Gosh! That all looks very lovely," said Lois dutifully.

Actually, she thought that Mum and Joan had chosen very well. "I wouldn't mind that silver star brooch myself. How much is it, Mother?"

"Oh, we haven't worked out prices yet," said Gran. "I am going round to Joan's this evening to sort it all out. We reckon on a one-third profit. What do you think, Mrs. Trinder? This is just for fun, and making a little bit on the side. Nothing like the pyramid wallahs."

After they had packed the jewellery carefully, and handed over a card to pay for it, Gran and Mrs. Trinder had a nostalgic chat about the days when Gran and family had lived in town. Then Lois led the way out of the shop and into a darkening twilight.

The car was parked on the wrong side of the road, and Lois walked round to open the rear passenger-side door.

"Lois!" shouted Joan, as she was about to get in to drive them home. "Lois, look out! Car coming fast behind you!"

"Lois!" shrieked Gran. "Watch out! Come back here!"

Too late to move, Lois flattened herself against the car and covered her ears. A terrible squeal of brakes caused her to press herself even harder as the whine of an engine out of control reached her.

Then it was gone, with much revving of the engine and angry hooting.

"Oh my God, what a wicked thing to do. Are you all right, Lois?" said Gran.

Lois was not all right, but she made a big effort and said she had caught sight of the driver. "One of Tresham's finest, I reckon! That gang of louts always around the Purple Dog. Out of control. He'll kill somebody, sure as eggs is eggs. If he doesn't kill himself first."

"Let's get home, Joan. I've had enough for one day," said Gran. "Thank God we don't live in Tresham anymore. At least we can walk down the street in Farnden without being mown down. Or can we?"

Lois knew her mother was thinking about her own narrow escape in the dark night so recently. "Real bad luck, Mum. But we shall be fine now, shan't we, Joan? We'll get Derek to give us a restoring cup of tea, and then we'll look at your lovely jewellery. Very well chosen, you two," she added, hoping to change the subject.

As Lois and the two others walked into the kitchen at Meade House, they found Derek talking to a tall man with his back to them. He turned, and Lois said flatly, "Inspector. How did you know?"

Derek held up his hand. "Not yet, Lois. Not until we're all safely settled in Gran's warm kitchen with a glass of something in front of you."

The first thing Cowgill said was that they had picked up the young idiot. He was doing one hundred miles an hour along the straight stretch out of Tresham. Drunk and belligerent.

"Did Mr. Trinder tell you, Inspector, what had happened?" said Joan.

"Yes, they called us as soon as you had gone. Fortunately, John Trinder has a photographic memory, and knew the number plate. Car stolen, of course."

After that, Joan shook her head, refusing the whisky, saying she had to drive on home. "Only round the corner, I know, but we all had the fright of our lives, and if I'm driving even a short distance, I shall not touch a drop."

Not bound by Joan's vow of temperance, the rest sipped and gulped and felt a whole lot better afterwards. Lois realised they must all be suffering from shock, and asked her mother to make cups of tea all round. "Plenty of sugar, too, please," she added.

They each gave their own account of what they had seen, ending with Gran, who took a deep breath and said, "I think I've seen him before."

"What? What do you mean, Mum?"

"Like what I said. I'm fairly certain it was the young fool who sent me flying into the field down the road, and you rescued me."

Inspector Cowgill frowned. "Could you see him clearly that night? I thought there was a lot of spray as he came towards you. It must have been difficult to see inside the car."

"Yes, it was. But I remembered at once that he had his hair done in a funny kind of hairdo brushed up. All the lads have it now. It's the latest fashion."

"In that case, how can you be sure it's the same chap?"

"Well, I am. But if you want to be sure, Inspector, maybe you could show me a photo of the youth you caught up with, and I can tell you if it's the same."

FORTY-FIVE

❧

LOIS HAD SPENT MOST OF YESTERDAY IN A KIND OF LOOP OF thoughts. She would have to stand by her promise to report to Cowgill. What should she tell him without all hell breaking loose in the police station? Her new friendship with Gloria, if she could call it that, would alarm him, no doubt. But Lois was convinced it could be productive. Already she had had a call from Gloria. Not particularly friendly, but very interesting.

The doorbell had interrupted her thoughts, and Gran had admitted Douglas with his two children, saying he was father and mother today as Susie had wanted to go alone to visit her sick sister.

They had stayed for lunch and tea, and then, after they had gone, Lois began to think again. The loop had finally ended when she fell asleep, but as it was still there when she awoke, she decided she would get to see Cowgill first thing, and be back in time for the team meeting at noon.

Now, fortified by one of Gran's working-day breakfasts, she dialled his number, and was pleased to hear him.

"My Lois, you must have been up with the lark, whose voice, though sweet, is not as sweet as yours. To my ear, anyway!"

"Cut the rubbish, please. Can you see me in about half an hour's time? I need your help in deciding what to do. I can't come to the station, so could we meet somewhere private?"

"Lois! Are you serious?"

Lois was losing patience. "Of course I am. It is to do with Aurora Black, and her unlovely husband."

"Ten thirty. I'll be waiting for you in our usual café, but ask them to show you to a back room. Mention my name."

"Fine. I'll be there. Oh, and actually I do have a reasonably acceptable singing voice. Back row in the sopranos in the Tresham Choral Society."

"Good heavens, is there no end to your skills, my clever Lois?"

Lois arrived at the café as the Town Hall clock struck half past ten, and as she came up to the counter, the girl manning the till hailed her in a loud voice.

"Morning, Mrs. Meade! The inspector is here already. Come this way, please."

So much for a private assignation, thought Lois. She shrugged, and hoped that Gloria or one of her friends had not seen her disappearing into a back room that smelt strongly of fish.

"Ugh! What a disgusting pong," she said, sitting perched on the edge of a plastic folding chair that threatened to collapse beneath her.

"Can't be too choosy in this job," said Cowgill. "Let's get out of here as soon as possible. Meanwhile, what's new?"

"It's to do with Aurora. Apparently, Donald Black was an even nastier character than we already thought. Almost as soon as they moved here, he began what can only be called the humiliation of Aurora Black, with his public assignations with other women. Sylvia Fountain was the only one at first, and was, so far as I know, the longest survivor."

"Are you telling me he killed other women and Sylvia was the last of the line?"

"No. I am only telling you what I know. I can't tell you my source. But Donald made no attempt to hide his affairs from Aurora. Sylvia idiotically fell for him, and she would do anything he asked. It must have been an awful time for Aurora. I wonder if this is why they moved here. But, of course, the problem moved with them. She must have been permanently on edge, with customers coming into the shop with knowing smiles. You know what gossips are like."

She was silent, and finally he said, "Is that it, then? You haven't risked being asphyxiated by fish pong to tell me only that?"

"No. This is the important bit. Linked to that. I am assured that the reading of the last will and testament of Donald

Black will be a big step forward in our investigations. And
no, I haven't told Derek or Mum that I was coming here. I
must get back home now. Team meeting at noon."

"Of course. Now, come with me and I'll show you the
back way out of here. And thank you, Lois. I can only say
how very grateful I am. This thing about the will is important, and I will act straightaway."

ON THE WAY HOME, LOIS WONDERED HOW EXACTLY COWGILL
was going to act. She supposed the police would be allowed
to look at wills, even before the beneficiaries. Something to
check.

She arrived home as Dot Nimmo was parking outside,
ready for the meeting.

"Morning, Dot! Unlike you to be first."

Dot frowned. She knew that she was usually the last,
but this morning she had a piece of news for Mrs. M, a private and important piece of news, she hoped.

Lois looked at her watch. It was a quarter to twelve, and
she ushered Dot into her study. "I need to go upstairs," she
said. "Shan't be long."

"Can it wait?" said Dot. "Please. I've got something to
tell you before the others get here."

"Fine. Carry on, Dottie."

"Well, my friend who works at the Mill said she didn't
want to be mixed up with the police. Her husband would
kill her, she said. So I promised not to mention her name.
Anyway, she said she was working late the night Sylvia

Black was killed. She passed by her bedroom door, and heard sounds of a struggle. That's how she put it."

"Is she reliable?"

Dot nodded. "I'd trust her from here to Jerusalem," she said.

"I'll tell Cowgill, Dottie. Thanks."

"Well, she don't want nothing to do with it. Leastways, not unless it's something to help you, Mrs. M. I know you really like Aurora Black and would like to help clear up the whole business."

FLOSS WAS THE NEXT TO ARRIVE, AND THEN SHEILA AND THE others in a bunch. Hazel was last, apologising for being late, but saying she was interviewing a new client.

"Recommended by Mrs. Prentise," she said. "Another well-off widow from those posh houses in millionaire's row in Fletching."

"Sounds good," said Lois. "Thanks, Hazel. Now, shall we start with reports? Do you want to begin, Floss? How's it going with the Prentises?"

"Very well. Mrs. P has stopped following me around, which is nice. I think she trusts me now. Coffee's real and good, and I wash my hands with gorgeous soap from Covent Garden! I think that's about it. Oh no, I did actually meet the daughter, Gloria, again. I admired the little silver heart locket she was wearing, and she said she bought it from Mrs. Weedon at the agricultural show. I'd love to see who she's hiding in there!"

Ann Purser

"So would I, Floss. So would I," said Lois.

The rest of the meeting went smoothly, and before they all started to move out, she asked them to sit down again as she wanted to ask a favour. "Of you all," she said

"Fire away," said Andrew. He had begun his decorating job in the Mill, and began to feel he knew the local environs well. He had spoken several times to Milly Black, and felt really sorry for her because she was clearly very worried about her mother.

"Well," said Lois, "it's like this. You must all be aware of the disappearance of Mrs. Black from the bakery. I would be most grateful if you could all keep eyes and ears open for any possible leads to finding her. Any mention of her or her husband. Or of Milly, come to that. The smallest thing may be useful. If you do hear or see anything, don't wait until next Monday meeting. Give me a ring straightaway. I have this odd feeling that there's something quite close to home that we haven't noticed."

"I might hear something at the Prentises," said Floss. "Mrs. P is always on the phone. Will that help?"

"Exactly that. Thanks, Floss. Anyone else?"

Andrew cleared his throat. "Um, well, I don't know if this has anything to do with Aurora's disappearance, but I have noticed in the hotel that the bedroom where the woman was strangled is permanently locked. I asked for a key, as I wanted to include it in my plan, but they said it had been locked, and they did not have a duplicate. The police, I suppose. All the other bedrooms have duplicate keys, and I know where they are kept. And that friend of Dot's was in there cleaning around. She's not exactly a ghostly sylph!"

Dot Nimmo laughed, and Lois joined in the general amusement.

"Perhaps they've got Aurora Black locked up in the bathroom," said Andrew.

"We're getting a bit wild here, I'm afraid," said Lois.

"I think it's probably got a bad-luck jinx on it now," said Hazel. "People coming in to the office in Tresham have mentioned the case a lot lately. They know our farm spreads quite a long way towards Brigham, and are curious to hear about the deaths there. I don't say much, but if I hear anything, I'll certainly pass it on, Mrs. M."

Sheila Stratford, whose husband was a retired farmworker, said that she would ask him if he'd heard any gossip in the pub, as he spent quite a long lunchtime there most days. Sheila was the one who was most willing to work over lunch hours, and had given him permission to meet his friends.

"You know I shall ask around the seamier sides of town," said Dot. "I think I know the right questions and the right people to ask. I hope you don't mind, Mrs. M, but I do have a hunch about something. I'd like to follow up a possible sighting of Aurora. I am not at all sure, but I think I caught a quick flash of the back of her outside the bakery, down a little alley at the side of the house, after she was supposed to have gone missing. I haven't reported it to the police, because I could not swear it was her, and anyway, they never believe a word I say. I can just hear old Cowgill: 'Don't waste our time, Mrs. Nimmo.'"

"I would like to know more about that, Dot. I'll see if anyone else has caught sight of her. That's the most optimistic thing we've heard."

"I'll go carefully, though. I'll let you know if I can find out more. Is that okay?"

"Keep in touch, promise? I'd rather you told us; then we can all help if it goes wrong."

"Don't forget I'm a Nimmo, will you? Nimmos hunt alone, like the dreaded panther."

This was so ridiculous that they all laughed, but kindly, and after that left in good order.

FORTY-SIX

❧

LOIS DECIDED TO COLLECT BREAD AND BUNS AFTER LUNCH, and to have a chat with Milly. When she told her mother this, Gran frowned disapproval.

"Why don't you come to the Women's Institute with me and Joan this afternoon, Lois?" said Gran, as she cleared the dishes from the table. There had been only she and her daughter having lunch, and Gran had thought Lois looked exhausted. She was surprised, as usually the team's meeting bucked her up, and after the girls and Andrew had all gone, Lois would often seem fired up and ready for anything. Today, all she looked ready for was bed.

"Thanks, but no thanks, Mum. I plan to go and stock up on bread and buns from Milly at the bakery."

"Oh, Lois, why don't you let Cowgill and his henchmen find Aurora? They're professionals, and it's only a hobby for you. A ridiculous hobby, as I've said many times. But I might as well save my breath." She put her arm round Lois's shoulders, and kissed the top of her head.

This was such an unaccustomed gesture that Lois looked at her mother's concerned face, and said she was very sorry for causing her worry, but she felt they were close to the end now, and she would take a long break from ferretin' after that.

"Don't stay over at Brigham too long then. Joan is coming to tea, and I know she'd like to see you. She's been dropping hints!"

"I'm always pleased to see Joan. Are you cooking up some other scheme?"

"Not necessarily. But we are a bit like you and your ferretin', my dear. Our intentions are good, but we seldom keep to them."

"True. Well, I know everyone enjoyed the last party, so maybe we can muster the troops and do it as a combined effort."

Gran nodded. "We hoped you'd say that. Well done, Lois. Your father would be proud of you."

"So where are you planning to have it?"

"At Mrs. Prentise's house. She's offered. She even said she would love to help and knew that all her rich friends would enjoy a gossip and the opportunity to buy."

"Does Floss know about this? She didn't mention it at the meeting."

"No, nobody else, except Joan and you and me. We'll get more supplies from our jeweller friends in Tresham, and second time round, we shall find it much easier. Correct the mistakes we made as beginners."

"Next stop a boutique in London's West End, I suppose?"

"Why not? Now, you go to Brigham and I'll go to the Women's Institute with Joan. And could you ask Milly to put this notice up in the shop?"

"Mum! You've been plotting this for days! And who did this notice for you?"

"Joan, of course. She's a whiz on the computer. Do you think I should get one? If she can master it, I'm sure I could do the same."

"Heaven preserve us! You'd have it on the muck heap before one week was out! Stay as sweet as you are, as the old song says. Now I must be off. See you at teatime."

THE SKY WAS GREY AND PROMISED RAIN, BUT THE NARROW ROAD to Brigham was empty of traffic, and Lois drove along slowly, appreciating time to get her thoughts straight. She could not ignore Dot's uncertain report that she might have seen Aurora, though she thought it well nigh impossible, and if she had, she might well be walking into some kind of trap. Her phone would not have stopped ringing if the poor woman had come home. So now she had to think of a way of asking Milly if she too had seen her mother.

The bakery had a closed sign in the window, and Lois rang the house bell. After a long interval, she tried again. She heard steps from the bakehouse, and then felt a soft hand on her arm.

"Mrs. Meade, how lovely to see you." It was Milly and she was outside, standing behind Lois, who quickly turned around.

"Hello, Milly! I came over hoping you'd have some bread left."

"Yes, and currant buns? I know Meades love currant buns. I came out here thinking I heard footsteps in the backyard. Ours is an old house, and we do have noises with no explanation. Anyway, enough of that. Come on in, and let's have a chat."

As they walked into the shop, Lois could now hear scuffling noises coming from the bakehouse. As Milly led the way through, Lois was astonished to hear her yell, one single high-pitched yell, and then see her crumple to the floor.

She rushed to help her, and in the space of a few seconds, Milly regained consciousness and sat up. She tried to say something, but only croaked one word, pointing to the oven.

"Mum!" she said again, and a figure stepped out of the shadows and rushed over to Milly.

"Aurora!" said Lois. "For God's sake, woman, where have you been?"

FORTY-SEVEN

ᴓ

BETWEEN THEM, LOIS AND AURORA HELPED MILLY TO A chair in the kitchen. Aurora thanked Lois over and over for helping her daughter, but Lois was concerned only with making sure Milly was fully conscious, and recovering from shock.

After a few minutes, Lois suggested she should leave them together, as they would have lots to talk about. She also intended to warn Cowgill that they should not have the police arriving too soon. It was possible, of course, that Aurora would vanish again, but Lois chose to ignore that possibility, risking Cowgill's wrath.

Milly and her mother both begged her to stay, but she felt that the two of them would have a lot to say that they would not necessarily reveal in front of her.

"I have to go now, but I'll pop over in the morning and

see that all's well. Lovely to have you back, Aurora, though I have to say you are not looking your usual calm and happy self. Now, no questions from me. I'll see you tomorrow."

She kissed each of them on the cheek, and left quickly. On the way home she stopped in a lay-by and called Derek on her mobile to give him the news. He replied that she was to go straight home and watch television or something to take her mind off things.

"Going to be difficult!" Lois said. "Will you be home early? I need some sensible advice. It is possible that Aurora will report to the police herself. But she seemed very far from her former self. Turned inward, if you know what I mean. And her voice was strained, and she looked awful."

Derek said worriedly that he was surprised Lois was able to tear herself away. He agreed that she should leave everything until tomorrow, and then wait to see what was going on before blundering in on something very odd indeed. And, he said, she should not mention it in front of Gran, as she was known to be the best purveyor of gossip in the village.

IT WAS NOT UNTIL GRAN HAD GONE UP TO BED THAT LOIS WAS able to tell Derek the full story. Not, as she said, that there was much to say. Aurora had appeared out of nowhere, and Milly had fainted from shock. They had all settled down eventually, and Lois was able to leave, somewhat unhappily. Aurora was looking very strange, and Lois worried about Milly's reaction.

Luckily, Derek was able to help her to a sensible conclusion by asking her to think herself into Aurora's place. Supposing she was not about to disappear again, there would be a lot of questioning for her to face. And, even more important, she would have to rebuild her relationship with her own daughter.

"They'll need time, poor things," he said. "I expect she will start baking again, and everyone around will find they need one of Aurora's stone-ground wholemeal loaves. At least it will be good for business."

"You are not saying she did it deliberately?" asked Lois fiercely.

"It's been known. Business not doing so well. An unexplained fire in an upper room, or a missing person in trouble with a hefty insurance claim. Aurora wouldn't be the first to be up to that dodge."

"There hasn't been a fire in an upper room."

"How do you know? How do you know Milly isn't in the same scam? How do you know anything at all about what goes on in Brigham Bakery?"

Lois was taken aback by this full frontal attack. She had thought Derek would give her calm advice on leaving mother and daughter to settle down and sort themselves out, ready to open the shop, do the baking and be nice to customers. What they would say would be up to them. There had been many questions Lois wanted to ask Aurora, but she instinctively gave way to the mother and daughter. First things first, and Milly's questions must come first.

"I suppose they could say Aurora had been in Brighton for a few days, revisiting places where she and Donald did their courting. When she was ready, she had come home, wanting to get back to normal, with the help of her charming daughter." Lois was beginning to feel irritated with both Aurora and Milly. Derek as always, enabled her to see more clearly. As far as any explanation was concerned, she was becoming suspicious. "Collusion" was the word that came to mind.

As soon as Lois had left, Milly began hysterically to accuse her mother of cruelty and selfishness. "Wherever you have been," she said, "you obviously didn't think of me at all. You just left! The trouble you have caused! Police! Friends! Everyone in Brigham. Even the hotel was overbooked with ghouls wanting to join in dredging the millpond."

To her horror, her mother had begun to laugh. "They did not dredge the millpond," Aurora said. "Come on now, Milly, you've done brilliantly well. I have been really proud of you. But that sniffer dog was useless! Although at one point I thought you would look up above where he settled and see the warm place above the oven. Was the dog Lois's idea?"

"No, it was Mrs. Tollervey-Jones's. At least, I think it was. Either hers or Gloria's. You remember Gloria?"

"Of course I remember Gloria. A bottle redhead. One of your father's little bits of fluff. I should have thought Gloria would not want me around, not after Donald was drowned and his ex-lover Sylvia was thought to be inheriting his estate . . ."

"What d'you mean? You'd be in the way? Oh, for heaven's sake, Mother, be sensible. I don't know where you've been, but you clearly need some tender loving care, so up to bed, and we'll talk later."

"Thanks, Milly love. I will go and have a rest. There'll be lots of sorting out to do tomorrow, I expect, but with you here to help, I'm sure I will get through it."

Milly took a cup of hot milk up to Aurora when she was in bed, and wished her sweet dreams. There was strain in her voice, and Aurora blew her a kiss and turned away.

Forty-Eight

❧

"WHERE'S SHE BEEN THEN? AND WHAT DID SHE HAVE TO say about causing so much trouble? That poor daughter of hers. I should think she was pretty sharp!" Gran looked as if she was about to fly off to Brigham and tackle Aurora herself.

"It wasn't at all like that," Lois said. She and Derek had agreed that they should give Gran an edited version of what had happened, but now she realised Gran would winkle out the whole thing in the end. Best to tell her now, before she concocted her own version. "We were going into the back kitchen for a cup of tea when Milly said she had heard a noise from the backyard. So we went into the bakehouse, and Milly yelled suddenly and her knees gave way and she fell. Then I saw it was Aurora, and she rushed with me to help poor Milly. After that, we calmed down, and when I was sure they were going to be okay, I left. That's it, Mum, straight from the horse's mouth."

"Mmm," said Gran. "So you don't know where that Aurora went and why? Well, thanks for giving me some of the facts, because without a doubt, the gossips will be busy with the whole thing, not to mention the police. I hope Cowgill sends our Matthew to see them. He's got such a good heart, bless him."

"And don't forget Josie in the shop," said Derek. "She'll be bombarded with questions. Let's hope business will be good, and she'll make a fortune in one day."

"That's all you think about! Money! I think everybody should leave the pair of them alone for a bit to sort themselves out . . ." Before she could finish her sentence, the phone began to ring, and she went off to her office to take the call.

"Cowgill? You haven't wasted any time. I was going to call you after we've finished our breakfast."

"Sorry, Lois. I had a call from an unnamed informer that the woman at the bakery was back and had been seen through the window. Another solid citizen called and claimed they had seen a light in the shop window, and there she was, the missing Mrs. Black."

"Why are you calling me, then?"

"Strangely enough, because I thought I would be giving you the good news."

"I was there when she reappeared. Seems there was a secret hiding place—maybe a kind of priest hole?—above the oven, and that's where she went. And where Henry refused to leave. Poor Aurora. Panic attack times six. Couldn't bring herself to come out again until she did eventually. Maternal instinct finally triumphed!"

"Quite right. So I shall be going along there this afternoon, and I'd be glad if you could find time to meet me there. About three o'clock, shall we say? I'd really appreciate it, Lois."

"Is that an order, nicely wrapped up?"

"However you like to take it, Lois love. See you later."

A wily old fox, thought Lois. He may be partly retired, but he knows what he's doing. Most of the time. She returned to the kitchen, and told Derek and Gran.

"What about going with Joan and me to the jewellers? Mrs. Prentise asked if she could come along and choose the stuff with us. She hoped Gloria would be free, too."

"Could you put it off until tomorrow? I would really love to come along."

Gran sniffed. She would have to ring round the others. But Lois had a ferretin' look in her eye, which alone would be sufficient warning that whatever she planned to do this afternoon would come first.

AT A QUARTER TO THREE, LOIS SET OFF FOR BRIGHAM. COWGILL was there before her, and Milly and Aurora were obviously not surprised to see her.

"I have told Milly and her mother that you would be coming, Lois. I think you may be able to help in remembering things that perhaps in the extraordinary nature of Aurora's disappearance may be forgotten."

Milly nodded, and Aurora looked as if everything was so confusing that Lois's presence was welcome. Cowgill said that they would begin at the beginning, the day when Milly first discovered her mother had gone.

Milly cleared her throat and reached for her mother's hand. She began when her mother did not come home when expected, and how she had gradually worried more and more. Then, when her mother did not appear again, she thought of a million things that could have happened to her. Lois had been very helpful, and Milly described how she had tried to get the bakery going again.

"And baked some very good loaves," said Aurora proudly.

"How do you know that, Aurora?" said Cowgill.

"Because she is my daughter, and has always been a lovely, talented girl," she answered. Except that she hadn't really answered, Lois decided. She said nothing, and waited while Cowgill tried and failed to get some hard facts from Aurora.

Finally, he turned to Lois and said he realised she would be going over the same ground as Milly, but could she describe in detail the shocking moment when Aurora reappeared?

The whole episode was so clear in Lois's mind that she was able to give a very detailed account, starting from when Aurora appeared like a dark shadow from the bakehouse and Milly had understandably fainted. Cowgill stopped her there, asking how Aurora had seemed. Was she confused, or injured in any way? Had she mentioned, even casually, or given any indication where she might have been? Had other people been involved? Had she been sleeping rough, and if so, where, and under what bridge?

At that point, Aurora, who had seemed in a daze still,

said the inspector should not question Lois about these things, as she was not, of course, able to answer them, since only she, Aurora, could know what happened to her, and she was about to tell them.

"I had been feeling quite rough since Donald was murdered, and thought I should probably take it easy for a bit. But then I had no idea that I was really sick. The afternoon I disappeared, Milly had gone shopping, and I couldn't face the dentist. Terror, I think. I felt sick, and I thought I would do what the old baker used to do, which was crawl into the warm space above the oven, completely out of sight. It has an exit under the eaves with a let-down rope ladder to the ground outside in the yard. That's been rolled up and forgotten. No one knew about the warm space except me, and I knew I would not be disturbed. Then, when I woke, I still felt odd. Frightened, really. I realised I could not go back into the bakehouse, nor could I bring myself to talk any more to Milly. The longer I stayed up there, the less able I was to confront anybody. I crept down the rope ladder when necessary, and made sure I wasn't seen.

"I suppose I knew what I was doing was stupid and wrong, but my courage had vanished. I was worried about my dear Milly, but could do nothing about it. I guess I needed some professional help, but was too scared to go out and find it.

"Finally, I realised that I had to face people. I could not secretly see my daughter bravely carrying on when it was in my power to make things all right again. So, like some evil zombie, I came down out of the warm space and frightened Milly to death. But not to death, thank God. We have had enough death, Inspector, and now you have your hard facts, and I have to find some way of repairing the damage I have done to my own daughter."

Silence engulfed them all, until Cowgill asked Lois if she had anything to add.

Lois then continued with her account up until this morning, when she had come to help. Things that Aurora had said now made sense of her conversation yesterday, and she added that her friend looked so fragile and unwell that it would be a good thing if the interview continued tomorrow.

Cowgill agreed reluctantly, and advised Aurora to get plenty of rest, as they would need to talk again. After he had gone, Lois insisted on making more tea, and settled Aurora in a comfortable chair in the tiny room that acted as an office for the bakery.

The three women, Aurora, Milly and Lois, were like hens on a perch, sitting in silence for half an hour. Aurora's eyelids gradually closed, and Lois could see she was sleeping peacefully. The shadow of a smile crossed her face every so often, and Lois guessed she was having pleasant dreams. Thank God, she thought, and wished she could be an invisible presence in those dreams.

FORTY-NINE

✳

GRAN HAD DULY FIXED A NEW TIME TO PICK UP JEWELLERY for the party at Mrs. Prentise's, and Joan collected Lois and her mother at eleven o'clock as arranged.

"Good news this morning, girls," said Joan. "That Aurora Black has come back home. I heard it this morning on the local news. It's so wonderful for that daughter of hers."

"Lois knows all about that," said Gran proudly. "She is a good friend of Aurora; aren't you, ducky?"

"Do you mind if I stop in Tresham for a couple of minutes while I drop a poster off with a friend who has a coffee shop?" Joan said. "It could be good publicity."

Lois and Gran said that was fine, but Lois thought their plan had been to restrict it to locals.

"True," said Joan. "But we could spread ourselves a little

more widely. Our first attempt was such a success, wasn't it, Elsie? And we can always stop the whole thing whenever we want to. The Prentises have gone separately, as it would have been a bit of a squash all together!"

They drove around town, and Lois was intrigued to see the coffee shop was across the road from, of all things, the Purple Dog, and outside was the fat man, staring at them. She was sure he recognised her, and felt a pang of alarm. Then they were off again, and up to the jewellers shop. They were welcomed in, and had a great time choosing sparkly brooches and coloured bead necklaces, silver bracelets and faux diamond rings. They had agreed to plough back into the business enough money to enable them to vary their stock, some expensive pieces but mostly cheap and cheerful. The jewellers were quietly amused at the growing confidence of the women, and asked them to stay for a coffee after business had been done.

Around half past twelve, they emerged from the shop, and Lois took one look at the car and gasped. "Oh my God, Joan, look at your tyres!" Then they all looked at the vicious slashing, and Joan burst into tears. Gran rushed to comfort her, and Lois set off at a trot around the narrow streets until she reached the Purple Dog. The fat man had disappeared, and all the doors and windows were shut. She crossed the street and marched up to the purple door, where she knocked and rang the bell. With little hope of being answered, she was surprised to see the door opening and the fat man staring at her.

"What do you want?"

"I think you know! I've come to tell you that I am going at once to the police and shall hold you responsible for slashing an innocent person's tyres. You may think you're boss around here, but the law of the land applies equally to the backstreets of this dump. *Especially* to the backstreets of this dump."

"Bog off," was the answer. "And take my advice. Keep your nose out of other people's business before you get seriously hurt. You and your family, Mrs. Nosey Parker Meade!" He was shouting now, and his face was suffused with an unpleasant puce colour.

She turned on her heel and marched off. When she arrived back at the shop, they were all sitting in the back room looking glum.

"I'm about to ring Inspector Cowgill," she said. "He'll deal with it."

"And don't forget your son-in-law, Lois," Gran said. She turned to the others. "My granddaughter is married to a policeman, you know."

"I don't see how that gets us home with a load of valuable jewellery," said Joan, sniffing back her tears. "Is it something to do with your stupid investigations, Lois?"

"Probably," said Lois. She was thinking hard. Who knew they were making this trip today? Her own family, of course, and anybody else Joan had mentioned it to. Then she had an unpleasant thought. The Prentises. Mrs. Prentise and Gloria had come with them, but in a separate car. They would not be risking slashed tyres themselves. No, Gloria was too highly placed in the netherworld of Tresham.

Could it have been a sudden decision of the fat man to muster his troops to do the deed? They would be very visible, but it was entirely possible that the rest of the street knew better than to cross members of the Purple Dog.

"What do you say, Lois?"

"Sorry? I was miles away. Sorry."

"I said we could get Derek to organise our rescue. Joan says her usual garage will come and collect the car, or put new tyres on it, so she can drive home. But it might take a while."

Lois immediately dialled Derek, who said he would be along to pick them up straightaway. "He said we were to keep our chins up, and he would give each of us a nice hug."

Joan laughed. "Trust your Derek to cheer us up," she said. "You don't know how lucky you are, Lois."

"I need to be lucky, Joan. And I am truly sorry if the slashing was directed at me. As a warning, maybe?"

WHEN THEY WERE ALL HOME AND RESTORED, GRAN RUSTLED UP an instant lunch, and Joan raised her glass of water in a toast to their rescuer, Derek.

"We need to have a sensible talk, girls," he said, "about all this jewellery business, and also Lois and the Brigham affair. Tell us honestly, Lois; do you think today's little episode was aimed at you? A crude attempt to stop you ferretin'?"

"Yes," Lois said baldly.

"Right. Then as from today, you will let Aurora Black

sort out her own troubles without your help. No more con-
ferences with Inspector Cowgill, and make this your last
jewellery party."

"It's not my party. I only make the tea. And if Mum and
Joan don't want my help, then fair enough. I'm not offering."

Gran and Joan chorused that of course they wanted Lois.
They said they had noticed that she was very good at helping with sales when buyers were queuing up.

After that, Joan went off to ring her garage to see when
she could pick up her car. Derek immediately offered to take
her back into Tresham, and a slightly shaky equilibrium was
restored.

FIFTY

꒳

G LORIA HEARD THE TELEPHONE RINGING AS SHE HELPED
her mother out of the car, and she fumbled with her
keys to open the elaborate security system in their house.

The phone had stopped ringing as she reached out a
hand to answer it. "Damn!" she said, waiting for another
attempt. When it came, it was blunt and to the point.

"Job done, Gloria," a man's voice said. "The lads enjoyed
it! Be in touch."

Gloria was silent.

"I think we did a good deed this afternoon," the voice
continued.

"You blithering idiot!" said Gloria. "I told you to back off.
I need Lois Meade more than she needs me at the moment.
So no more damage! Got it?"

*   *   *

GRAN AND JOAN, AFTER A LUNCHTIME OF GOOD INTENTIONS AND private determinations, decided to take the jewellery round to Joan's and do a bit of pricing and sorting. They both loved this job, and a lot of time was spent trying on pieces that they fancied for themselves.

"Not that we ever intend to *have* them for ourselves," Joan said now, extending her hand with spread-out fingers to see how a large imitation sapphire looked.

"Of course not," said Gran. "Anyway, our hands are too knobbly and blue-veined to wear show-off rings. I think we'd better to stick to brooches pinned on a black cashmere jacket. Did you notice Mrs. Prentise? I reckon that duo have got plenty of dough between them. Do you like them, Joan? My Lois and Gloria seem to have a sort of friendship. How about Mrs. Prentise?"

Joan sniffed. "I wouldn't trust her as far as I could throw her. All smiles and touchy-feely, too. Have you noticed how she puts her hand on your arm when she's talking to you? And the next minute cold as ice. I can't be doin' with that!"

"Why do you suppose she's offered her house for a party? Most unlikely that she needs a cut of the profits. In fact, Joan, we ain't discussed that at all, have we? I suggest we offer her 10 percent."

"Whatever you say, Elsie. She hasn't mentioned it at all, so far, but I doubt if she's doing it out of the goodness of her heart! Something to do with her daughter, do you think?"

"Could be," said Gran. "More probably something to do with *my* daughter. I don't suppose she'll take any notice of Derek's orders. Never has, in my experience."

LOIS HAD BEEN IN HER OFFICE ALL AFTERNOON, MAKING TELE-phone calls and sorting absentmindedly through New Brooms papers. It had been such a strange day. The trip to the Trinders' jewellery emporium had been a pleasant interlude, with Gran and Joan so excited, and the Prentises being modest and not at all patronising, considering they could have probably bought up the entire shop's stock without batting an eyelid.

Then the tyre slashing, and Derek rescuing them. But at lunchtime, she could see that he was really upset and worried underneath his masterful mask. Goodness, how patient he had been over the years since she had first taken to ferretin' with Inspector Cowgill! Not only patient, but most of the time concealing his angry jealousy of the top cop, who made no secret of his admiration of Lois.

She sighed. Perhaps it was time to consider retirement? More thinking to be done there. Lois's attention was taken suddenly by the squeal of brakes in the road outside Meade House. Then she saw the tall figure of her son Douglas marching up the drive. Glad of a break, Lois went immediately to the kitchen, where he had already kissed his grandmother, who had conveniently put a chocolate sponge cake on the table.

"Hi, Doug," Lois said. "How's our son and heir? So nice to see you, love. Is this a social call, or do you have an ulterior motive?"

Douglas grinned. "Both," he said. "Susie and I were thinking we need a weekend break, far away from the daily round of children and work."

"And you'd like us to take charge. It would be lovely if the two tinies could come here. Jeems is good with children, and they really like her. We could do a good job of babysitting, Mum, couldn't we?"

Suddenly the idea of having to concentrate on a couple of small children seemed a really good idea.

"You read my mind, Mum," said Doug. "Would you really have them for us? We'd be away for two nights only. Susie fancies a weekend in Paris, and I'm rooting for Iceland. What do you think will win?"

"Paris," chorused Gran and Lois. "You'll love it."

"Well, that's really nice of you both. Susie will be so excited, and so will the children. But what about Dad? Is he around?"

"No, he's back at work. But we'll tell him at teatime. Can you stay? We can take Jeems for a walk in the woods."

"I'd love to do that, Mum, but it'll have to be a quick one. I have to check in at work at some point. You can understand that, I'm sure."

"As nobody has asked me to join the walk," said Gran, "I shall go to see Josie in the shop. We can have a nice chat before the school bus gets in. After that she's busy for the rest of the afternoon. So off you go, now. Lovely to see you, Douglas."

THE SKY WAS OVERCAST WHEN DOUGLAS AND LOIS SET OFF, BUT by the time they reached Farnden Hall, the clouds had cleared and the sun was warm on their backs. The souvenir shop was busy, and they walked on round the back of the house and into the woods.

"I've a new signpost for them," said Douglas, as they let Jemima off the lead. She set off immediately into the thicket to find rabbits.

"What? Terriers Forbidden?"

"No. Giraffes: Bend or Bump. It is all rather ludicrous, isn't it, Mum?"

Lois agreed. But said she supposed they were harmless.

She could not remember the last time she and Douglas had been able to talk without interruption, and they had a great time, chatting away about Susie's intention of going back to work part-time and the brilliance of the children at their respective schools. Lois also gave him an edited account of the attack on Joan's car, and her own experience of being closely buzzed by a young idiot. "Dangerous, it was, son. Makes you wonder what those tearaways do for innocent fun! Time to turn around, I think, Doug," she added. "You said around fourish, didn't you? We'll put Jeems back on the lead, and then walk smartly back. And yes, I will take great care in future. Why else do you think I asked you to come for a walk in the woods?"

FIFTY-ONE

✤

Next morning, Derek and Lois were having breakfast when the phone rang.

"It's Aurora Black for you, Lois," Derek said in a tight
voice. "Shall I tell her you're out?"

"No, of course not. Aurora is my friend, and I don't ditch
friends in a hurry. Besides which, she would have been busy
all yesterday afternoon at the bakery."

She took the call in her office with the door closed. "Hi,
Aurora. How are you and Milly?"

"We're fine," Aurora said, and at once Lois could hear that
she was much better. "I spent hours yesterday in the bakehouse. There's nothing to beat a session of kneading the
dough to clear the head! Can you come for a coffee this morning? It would be lovely to see you again."

"Um, can I just check my diary? I'll ring you back in a few minutes. So glad to hear you sounding back to normal."

She returned to the kitchen to face concerted disapproval from Derek and Gran.

"You must be mad, Lois," said Derek. "If you are seen visiting Aurora, you'll be courting trouble. Surely you realise someone wants to stop you ferretin' and intends to succeed, one way or another?"

"Hear, hear," said Gran. "Please, Lois, think of the rest of your family. Don't they mean more to you than your new friend?"

"She's not new. Not very, anyway. And yes, of course I think of the rest of you all the time. But I don't actually think my seeing Aurora for a cup of coffee is going to trigger a morning of armed conflict in Brigham. Added to that, the eminent Inspector Cowgill is coming at three o'clock this afternoon to have a conference. So if these idiots are following me around, they'll surely be put off by the visible presence of a top cop protecting me."

Derek sighed deeply. He looked at Gran, and said, "I give up. We shall just have to trust you to be sensible. Okay, Gran?"

He could see that Lois had a mutinous expression developing, and so said he must be off to work, leaving her to a sparring match with her mother.

THE DRIVE OVER TO BRIGHAM GAVE LOIS TIME TO THINK, AND now that Aurora was clearly functioning much more normally, she considered a few questions that she would want to ask her.

Not an inquisition, of course, but slipped into the conversation. Milly was apparently still at home, and helping out with the baking, also giving her mother time to recover properly.

Milly. She was a lovely girl, and clearly devoted to Aurora. But when she was growing up at home, she must have witnessed how her parents got on together. If Gloria's story of the Sylvia association was true, wouldn't it have been difficult to conceal at least some acrimonious conversations between Donald and Aurora? But it was possible, only just possible, that Aurora did not know what was going on under her nose. No, not possible.

She must have known, and decided to ignore it.

And Gloria. How much could she believe what Gloria had told her? She seemed to wish to extricate herself from any relationship with Donald. No one would necessarily know the truth, except Sylvia, Donald and Gloria. And Gloria had tried to convince her that the Purple Dog was an innocent drop-in centre, or knocking shop, as Derek used to call it, and her cousin Sylvia, who worked there, had had a special relationship with Donald Black. Gloria was determined to discover who killed her cousin, and if it was Donald, the wicked sod, then who killed him?

It was a completely different Aurora who met Lois at the bakery door. Pink cheeks, a big smile and hands covered in flour.

"Come on in," she said. "I am so glad to see you. I realise I have worried not only my daughter, but a lot of friends in the last few days, and I think I have apologies to make. But coffee first. Milly has gone to the village shop to see a friend, so we can have a nice twosome break!"

After coffee and buns had done their work, Lois leaned back in her chair and said, "Right, explanation time. Take it gently, Aurora."

"Well, Milly has heard it all now, of course. And I gave as accurate an account as I could to Inspector Cowgill. Up to where I stumbled into the bakehouse. That's when you saw me, you and Milly. The rest you know, Lois."

"And goodness, what a sad tale it is! But never mind, Aurora dear, you have been seriously sick, and must let us help you, if we can. And the doctor said not to worry, thank heaven. Now, let's talk about how you survived in an airless warm box room without any of us finding you."

Aurora managed a smile, and said she had discovered this dark chamber above the bread oven when they first moved into the bakery. Not only was it hidden by a movable flour bin, so that the sleepers would not be disturbed—that was in the old days, of course—but once you were up there you could push a heavy old wooden flap across so it was just about invisible.

"Why did you never tell us about this hideaway?"

Aurora hesitated. "I liked to keep it a secret. There is a way of getting out of it into the yard, but it is all overgrown with thick holly bushes. I did manage to push my way through once or twice, but it was dark and I got torn to pieces by the thorns. Look! I managed to get what I wanted when Milly was in bed. Bread and water. I slept a lot of the time, and was a bit dopey when I finally emerged. I was totally at a loss when I saw Milly collapse.

"The thing is, I've always managed to pretend to Milly, and to others, that my marriage was a happy one. It wasn't, of course. Donald was a serial Don Juan, only rather smaller than the original. He had a girl in every town he visited, and where there wasn't a local tart to be had, he would send for Sylvia Fountain."

"Oh, Aurora, how dreadful for you! Did he tell you about them?"

"Oh yes. In detail. That was adding spice to infidelity. Then there was perhaps the hardest thing to bear. When he was at home for a few days, he would have an arrangement with Sylvia whereby she arrived at the Mill House Hotel with her brother, who left in due course, usually in darkness, and Sylvia would signal to Donald that it was safe to come over. Donald would be in a spare room overlooking the hotel, pretending to sleep on his own because of a bad headache. Of course, I knew exactly what was going on, and he knew that I knew. And worst of all, I knew that he had willed all his estate, including the shop and business, to Sylvia Fountain. He boasted about that, too. Used it as a weapon against me if I complained. Oh God, Lois, how I hated him!"

FIFTY-TWO

᠅

COWGILL CALLED AS PLANNED TO CHECK THAT LOIS WAS ALL right, and to see what she had gleaned from her conversation with Aurora.

"Well, you seem to have everything in hand," she said, "so there's not a lot of ferretin' for me to do, is there?"

She did not admit to Cowgill that there was actually a lot more ferretin', and not far from home. In spite of all Aurora's unburdening, she felt strongly there was more to discover.

"I am sure Derek and Gran would heartfeltly agree! We have no idea yet who strangled Sylvia Fountain or put Donald Black into the water at the Mill House Hotel."

Cowgill raised his eyebrows. "Correct, my dear, but we are much further along the road to finding out. Now, I must go and let you get on." He stroked Jemima with an elegant hand. Good fingernails, Lois noticed. And a gentle touch. She shook herself. Quite enough of that, Lois Meade! she said to herself, and opened the office door to let Jeems trot back to the kitchen.

WHILE LOIS AND COWGILL WERE IN CLOSE CONFERENCE, GLO-ria was also making headway. But she was operating alone, and was beginning to wish she had someone to talk to about what she had discovered. She had the deal made with Lois Meade, but she wasn't sure she trusted her. Too pally with that Cowgill. But, in the end, she realised, she would need police cooperation to bring the perpetrator to justice.

Sylvia had been asleep fully dressed when strangled. Gloria was sure about that. Her cousin was a big girl, and had always been the sporty one. She had even tossed the caber on a visit to Scotland one year! She would have found it easy to beat off any attacker if she was awake.

Unless she had been knocked out first? Physically knocked out, or with some kind of anaesthetic! That must be it. The silver necklace was perhaps already worn by Sylvia. The strangulation could have been an intended distraction. How could she find out? Only by asking someone who had been in on the results of the postmortem. Lois Meade? She was close to Inspector Cowgill, who would surely have had all the information to hand.

She took out her mobile and dialled Lois's number.

"Damn, she's not there!" she said and left a message saying she would ring again later.

FIFTY-THREE

✢

JOAN AND ELSIE HAD BOOKED THEIR JEWELLERY PARTY OVER at Mrs. Prentise's for two days, and now, with everything necessary to make things go with a swing, all except for the jewellery itself, they set out at nine o'clock in the morning ready for anything.

Lois had agreed that she and Derek would take all the jewels over tomorrow, so that there would be no worries about safety overnight. Lois would not admit it, but she was glad Derek had agreed to accompany her, even though he kept up a kind of mantra stressing that this was the last time anybody in his family had anything to do with this foolish venture.

"Two elderly ladies," he had said at the breakfast table this morning, "with one reluctant daughter and a small white dog. You'd not be a match for anyone if there was trouble."

"I fail to see how we could be in trouble in a crowded private house, where our jewellery is cheap and cheerful and when a police constable in uniform just happens to be around, ostensibly to buy a birthday present for his wife."

"You mean Matthew?" Derek could not believe that Lois and Gran could possibly have organised their own personal police presence. He supposed that Cowgill must have something to do with it. He knew, regretfully, that Lois could wind the inspector round her little finger.

"Yes, I mean Matthew, and his boss knows all about it," Lois said, reading his mind.

"Nevertheless, I intend to go with you tomorrow," he said. "Are you following Joan and Elsie over this morning?"

"I said I would call in a bit later. I have one or two calls to make, and admin to attend to. I promised to take them a sandwich lunch and stay on for a bit. You will want to swell the ranks of our bodyguard tomorrow, I suppose?"

"Lois, provided you agree that this is the last foolish enterprise that anyone in my family is involved in, then I will give up going to Tresham to follow my favourite team and come with you. That's how seriously I take this whole business."

Lois kissed him lightly on the cheek. "You've forgotten something," she said.

"Don't raise my hopes," he said, putting his arms around her.

"No, silly. I'm thinking of Gran. She never tires of telling us that she is connected only by marriage—ours—and her name is Elsie Weedon, and not Meade. And that means that she is not under your jurisdiction. Her own boss, in other words. But as always, we shall do our best to keep her safe."

*   *   *

AFTER A CHAT WITH HAZEL IN TOWN, AND VISITING A COUPLE OF
potential New Brooms clients, Lois walked round to a big
barn building at the back of the Prentises' house in Fletching. This barn had been generally smartened up where for
ten years or so Mrs. Prentise had run an art gallery. This had
been very useful for moving on stuff, but she had tired of it
and wound up the business.

Lois found Mrs. Prentise, Gran and Joan, and Gloria Prentise, all sitting with plates on their laps, helping themselves
to assorted sandwiches and coffee from an elegant trolley.

"Come in, Mrs. Meade!" said Mrs. Prentise. "We are taking a lunch break. Please take a plate and help yourself.
There's plenty for all. Mrs. Black at the bakery prepared a
spread for us, and will be coming back to clear away the
debris. I must say I am very relieved to see her back home
safe and well. Don't you agree, Gloria?"

So much for my ham rolls and pickle, thought Lois, and
put them back in her bag. Mrs. Prentise turned to her daughter, who was handing around small strawberry tartlets.

"Oh yeah," said Gloria. "We're delighted to see her back,
aren't we, Mrs. Meade?"

Having got Lois's attention, she winked at her and
beckoned her towards the kitchen.

"What's the secret?" Lois was not at all sure she wanted
to be seen cosying up to a Prentise, but Gloria said she had
had serious thoughts about the actual murder of her cousin
Sylvia. She realised that when she was killed, it was not
actually with the necklace as weapon. That, she said, was

an attempt at a cover-up, and, so far as Gloria could discover, it had worked.

"Sylvia could easily have seen off any attack on her. No, I reckon she was killed in some other way, then put into the bed and the necklace tightened to look like strangulation."

"Are you sure about that?" Lois felt a shiver down her spine. This was a very plausible explanation, and one which had not perhaps been expected to emerge. The necklace was the obvious one. Full stop. "I suppose the only way of checking is to find out what the postmortem produced. And that means asking."

"Exactly," said Gloria. "And you are well in with top-cop Cowgill. Can you ask him, and let me know? He'd never talk to me, nor do I want him to. But you are the best person for the job. So when can you see him?"

"Hey, hold on a minute. I need to do some thinking. Then, if I think it is appropriate, I will contact him."

Gloria looked at her and shrugged. "No need to be so stuffy, Lois. I bet you cannot even spell 'appropriate'! Still, beggars can't be choosers, so I'll wait to hear from you."

Lois roared with laughter. "I deserved that," she said finally. "And thanks for letting me know what you think really happened. Does it seem possible that Sylvia had gone to sleep and so wasn't alert enough to know what was happening to her, especially if she had gone to bed *wearing* the necklace? I remember she was found fully dressed."

Mrs. Prentise looked at the two returning, and raised her eyebrows. "What are you two up to, Gloria?" she said.

Before Lois could reply, Gran answered for her. "Checking on Floss's work around the house, I expect," she said.

"My daughter is most particular about the standard of New Brooms work. All well, Lois?"

"Yes, Mum, thanks. Floss is very reliable, as are all my girls."

"I understand you have a young man also on your books? Working on a new colour scheme for the hotel in Brigham? I may have some such interior decor for him, when he's available." Mrs. Prentise dabbed the corners of her lips to remove any traces of cream.

"Fine," said Lois. "I'll send him over to see you at your convenience. And thanks. Andrew is very good at keeping separate the two strings to his bow!"

AFTER JOAN, GRAN AND LOIS HAD FINISHED AND GONE HOME, Gloria was left with her mother. They collapsed into deep armchairs and sipped a long gin and tonic. "Ice and slice," said Mrs. Prentise. "Very restoring. I wonder who thought up that irritating name for it. G & T was what we used to call it. Very sophisticated, we all thought! Now, what were you and Lois Meade plotting in the kitchen?"

"I'm sick of plotting," Gloria said carefully. "We are no nearer discovering who killed Sylvia. The one person who we know might have had a motive was her precious Donald. Donald! What an idiot he was. But cruel, too. I know he and Sylvia weren't getting on too well. That Aurora Black must have known what was going on. They weren't particularly good at concealing it, and most of the village of Brigham knew. I don't like to think it, but Sylvia could have tried to blackmail him. Perhaps he wanted to give her up and she was desperate? Or, more likely, the other way round. She wanted to give him up, and they had a fight that went wrong."

"Well, I'll say this once, Gloria. We only think we know who killed Sylvia. She was killed before Donald died, and he could well have wanted her permanently out of the way for a reason such as you just mentioned. Be very careful if you are getting too involved. Two cruel and wicked murders is enough."

"Thanks, Mother. But don't forget Donald apparently had a dodgy alibi. At least, I think it was dodgy. Usual thing— bribe a friend to sleep in your bed with covers over his head, while you scarper down the motorway. So I will be careful. Not sure about Lois Meade. I'll keep a close eye on her."

FIFTY-FOUR

❧

WHEN LOIS WAS BACK IN HER OFFICE IN MEADE HOUSE, she began to think seriously about obtaining the results of the postmortem on Sylvia Fountain's body. She switched on her computer and entered 'postmortem.'" Amazing!" she said aloud, and then, "Disgusting!"

The number of results included ancient photographs of bodies in all states of completeness, and very touching ones—mostly Victorian—of whole families posing for the camera with a tiny, beautifully dressed baby in a coffin, surrounded by its living brothers and sisters.

Of course, she thought to herself, babies nowadays can survive most things, but in those days it was very different. Big families were the norm, with some of their number not expected to live to adulthood. Pneumonia took off many, she knew, from her own grandmother, who had lost two, one boy and one girl, in babyhood.

Not wanting to read or look at more, she narrowed her search to instructions on what happens when a postmortem is requested. When she came to the paragraph where it said that a close member of the family could ask for results of the autopsy, she stood up from her desk, yelling, "Yes, of course! Gloria!"

But would a cousin count as close family? She reckoned that if there were no other closer living relatives, Gloria would stand a good chance. She picked up her phone and dialled. "Hi! Gloria? Lois here. It's not Gloria? Well, where is she, and what are you doing with her phone? She's in the shower? Oh, sorry, Mrs. Prentise. Yes, of course I'll hold on."

After a minute or two, Gloria came on the phone, and listened to Lois's revelation. "My goodness," she said. "Fancy you discovering that! I'll get on to the coroner's office straightaway."

"Can I come, too?" said Lois. "I might not be able to be with you when you get the information, but you can tell me at once so as not to forget anything. We really need details, Gloria."

"I'll get back to you. Cheers."

Lois sat back in her chair, and thought of all the questions Gloria would need to ask. And then she grinned to herself.

Who would have thought that she would be in partnership with Gorgeous Gloria? She began to type.

She had no sooner begun to formulate questions than her phone rang, and it was Inspector Cowgill.

"Good day, Lois, my dear. How are we?"

"I don't know about you, but I am absolutely fine."

"Really! So something special has happened, has it?"

"Yes, and don't ask me what it is, because it is a secret."

"We deal in secrets, here in the police station. I'm all ears. And if you won't tell me, I shall be forced to have you brought in here in chains for a good old-fashioned grilling!"

"No chance," said Lois. "But I promise to tell you, if you promise to help us. Me and Gloria."

"Lois, um, I hate to ask, but have you been celebrating something? You sound very pixillated."

"Don't speak to me of pixies! Sounds more like you've been on the bottle."

"That word means excited. And I'll look forward to hearing from you after you've had a strong black coffee. You and Gloria—Prentise, I presume?"

"Do you promise to use your influence for us?" said Lois. But Cowgill had gone, and Lois realised that her attempt at corrupting a serving police officer had failed.

Next she redialled Gloria, and reported back, and then said she was to let her, Lois, know immediately when she had a yes or no from the coroner's office.

"Okay. Will do. But I have been thinking. Supposing a body gets cremated; won't that get rid of any physical evidence of what was responsible for the death?"

"It says here that if a body is sent for an inquest, by doctor or police, there can be no burial or cremation until it is released by the coroner."

"Well, we didn't hear nothing about being present at an inquest, if there was one."

"No layperson is allowed to be at an inquest, but you

can be represented. Are you sure there wasn't someone closer to her than you?"

Gloria then went into a long tale of how that branch of her family had slowly dropped off the perch, one by one, and some not by any means willingly. This reminded Lois of the criminal background of the Prentises, and she hoped that Gloria would not be regarded as an unreliable witness, when needed.

"Right," she said. "Thanks, Gloria. Let's see how you get on. I don't think my friend Cowgill is going to be much help to us. But I can always try. Good hunting, then."

She put down the phone, and it immediately started to ring again. It was the inspector again, and he said in a serious voice that Lois should be very careful about banding together with Gloria Prentise.

"I don't have to remind you, Lois, that her relations are a very crooked and clever lot. If you are not careful, she will use you, cooperate as far as it suits her, and then leave you in the lurch."

"I realise all that, Hunter. But thanks, anyway. And if you can look up records on any inquest held on Sylvia Fountain, and can bring yourself to let me know the results, then we might have something concrete to get us further on in our investigations. And by we, I mean you, me and Gloria. She is having a go at being Sylvia's nearest and only relation."

"Come and see me on Monday, and I might be able to help."

GRAN HAD GONE INTO OVERDRIVE IN THE KITCHEN, AND THE table was covered with wonderful homemade goodies.

"But I thought Aurora and Milly were doing the refreshments," Lois said, coming in to tell Gran she would be going into town next week.

"These are for a special little party for helpers after we close the doors tomorrow. It will be our last party, Joan and me have decided," Gran said.

Lois thought of saying she remembered Gran saying that last time. But not wanting to spoil the fun, she didn't, merely adding that if Mum wanted to go into town to the farmers' market, she would be happy to give her a lift.

"What are you doing going into town on a wash day?" Gran said accusingly.

"I have to see Inspector Cowgill," Lois said. "His suggestion, and I agreed. Always willing to give the police a hand, that's me."

"It just so happens," Gran said, "that on Monday the mouse man is coming to butcher all the little darlings behind the sofa and the piano, and in every other nook and cranny in this house. We are overrun, Lois, and it's no good asking Derek to do the job, because he has plenty of other things to do, and in any case is quite likely to say he'll use those trap things, where our mice go in and out at will."

"Phew, that's a long speech, Mother dear. Best, maybe, not to tell Derek until the mouse man is actually here."

FIFTY-FIVE

❧

NEXT MORNING, LOIS AND DEREK ARRIVED OUTSIDE Trinder's Jewellers without mishap, but Lois still felt happier with Derek's reassuring presence beside her.

The shop was busy, as the whole town of Tresham was in festive mood, with the balloon festival in full swing.

"I remember when I was little, I used to think they had party balloons hidden somewhere, when all the time it was the huge ones in the park, with baskets underneath and bursts of flame heating up gas, or something."

"Ah, so was it a great disappointment when you found out?"

"Oh no. My dad promised to take me in one of the big balloon trips when I was bigger. But he never did. Mum says he was scared."

"I expect our Gran would have gone on her own! Anyway we'd better get the goodies for the girls and take them back to Fletching. The sooner the better, Gran said."

Lois leaned over to the driving seat and kissed Derek on his stubbly cheek. "And the sooner you have a shave, the better," she said.

"MORNING, DEREK; MORNING, LOIS!" SAID JOHN TRINDER. "Everything's ready for Mrs. Weedon and her friend. I must say I do admire their pluck and determination."

"They say this is their last jewellery party," said Lois.

"Oh dear," said John. "We had hoped it would be a regular event."

"Naturally," said Lois. "I can see it is a nice little order for you! But we both think it is time to take life a little more easily for our Gran. Joan is a widow living alone, of course. But Gran is a full-time housekeeper for me and Derek."

"I wonder if you have thought that perhaps Mrs. Weedon is so good for her age *because* she is very active?" John Trinder smiled to soften what could be considered criticism. "Anyway, will you wish them the best of luck for today from us?"

"I have to come into town on Monday," said Lois, "so perhaps I will pop in and tell you how it went. I know there'll be one or two pieces which Mum wants to give to the hospice shop."

The two went back to Derek's van, and Lois looked nervously at the tyres. All blown up as correctly as the balloons now floating beautifully over their heads.

"Come on, Derek; let's get going. I shan't feel safe until

we've delivered this lot to Joan and Mum over at the Prentises in Fletching."

LOIS HAD TO HAND IT TO GLORIA AND HER MOTHER. TOGETHER with Joan and Gran, they had set out the jewellery so that it looked like a sale of the late Duchess of Windsor's valuables at Sotheby's. A few of the display tables from the days of the art gallery remained, and these had given the old building a professional air. Spotlights, too, gave extra sparkle to the jewellery.

"Lovely!" said Lois. "Now, shall I go and do duty in the kitchen? And Derek has suggested himself as a roaming undercover man."

"Don't worry, Mrs. Meade," said Mrs. Prentise. "Our family are really good at undercover work. We shall be fine, but if Derek likes to be an extra, I'm sure he'll be very welcome."

The idea of being an extra did not appeal to Derek, and he said he would do some useful work in the garden of the old lady next door, and they were to yell for him if necessary.

After a snack lunch, around half past one, last touches to the display were made, and Lois switched on her favourite jazz music turned down low. "Nothing worse than having to compete with loud background music," she said to Gran, who had stationed herself behind the display to be ready for the first buyers. Lois had to admit that her mother, smartly dressed in a black suit with white shirt, looked very efficient and attractive.

A respectable queue had formed outside the door, and Mrs. Prentise was ready to open up on the dot of two o'clock.

"Here we go, girls!" she shouted, and backed away to join Gran and Joan behind the table, big smiles of welcome on their faces.

First in the queue was Gloria. "Hi, Lois," she said. "What can I buy my elegant mother for her birthday? And how have you got on with you-know-who?"

Lois nodded. "Fine, thanks. I am to see him on Monday, so will know more then. Now, how about this lovely gold chain? Same pattern as rich old men used to wear across their chests in olden times."

"I don't particularly want to look like a rich, portly old man! I don't think much of your sales talk, Lois Meade!"

"You're right. How about a discreet pair of earrings, like little silver cushions with tiny real diamonds inset?"

"Definitely better. And yes, I'll take those. Can you put them in a pretty box, and I'll take them when everyone has gone? Put a red dot beside them, *pour encourager les autres*."

"Exactly. *Merci beaucoup*," Lois said, not to be outdone. "I'll be in touch."

Then, suddenly, the hall was full, and Derek appeared to tell her that a coachload of ladies, mature in years, had arrived outside. "Do you want extra help?" he said.

And then Josie arrived from the shop, and in no time, it seemed everyone was busy, and money was flowing into the safety cash boxes.

"Wow!" said Joan, when they finally managed to close and lock the door. "Four hours on me feet and not a single twinge! How about you, Elsie?"

Gran grinned. "Same here. What a wonderful afternoon, and where did all those women come from? That lot in a motor coach."

Matthew, wearing mufti, had come in with Josie, and Lois could see he was smiling broadly.

"Hi, Matt," she said. "You're looking cheerful. Day off?"

"Not quite," he said. "I was being helpful at the crossroads. A bus drew up, full of affluent-looking ladies out on an excursion. Their driver was young and new, and had lost the way. They were all desperate, and they asked where the nearest toilets were. I naturally directed them to the wonderful house with a jewellery sale on. I was sure Mrs. Prentise would allow them to use the gardener's loo."

"Which I did," said Mrs. Prentise, rubbing her hands. "And the desperate ones I sent upstairs to the spare room en suite. Now then, who's counting? If no one else wants the job, I'm volunteering."

Fifty-Six

WHEN ALL THE CASH HAD BEEN COUNTED TWICE, AND the few remaining pieces of jewellery packed carefully in boxes to take to the hospice shop, the party began. Husbands and wives of helpers swelled the numbers, Lois put on more cool jazz, and with the display units cleared to the sides of the barn, a generous area of empty floor remained.

After a glass or two of bubbly wine, Derek bowed lightly to Mrs. Prentise and asked if she would like to dance. She smiled kindly and said she happened to have a vintage disc of Victor Sylvester in her pocket. Thrilled, Derek moved out onto the floor, and the two, with considerable grace, performed a faultless quickstep to roars of applause.

This was followed by a wonderful waltz performed by Joan and Gran dancing together. "Stately as a galleon," muttered Derek into Lois's ear. "Should I ask Josie?"

"I think this had better be the last waltz, and Matthew will no doubt persuade his wife onto the floor. Which leaves me. How about it, boy?"

THE MEADES WERE NOW ALL GATHERED IN THEIR KITCHEN, conducting a postmortem on the evening's event. There was no doubt that jewellery sales had been a great success, and the takings were double that of their last fixture.

"Now, everybody quiet now," said Gran. "Me and Joan want to say something."

"Joan's in the kitchen," said Derek.

"That's why I'm going to say something. What we wanted to say was that we are really grateful to Lois. To everybody, of course, but a special thank-you from we two to Lois. In spite of disapproving of our doing the whole thing, she buckled to and put all her considerable energy into helping us. So thank you, me darling. Your dad would have been proud of you. And here, Lois Weedon, here is a small token of our gratitude."

By this time, there was much clearing of throats and mopping of eyes, Lois more than most. She took the pink box and opened it. "Oh, Mum, how lovely," she said and held up a gold chain with a pendant of a small dog, enamelled white with a scarlet collar.

Derek silently handed her his large handkerchief, and she wiped her eyes. Not long after, all were safely sent off in good order, and he and Lois retired to bed.

"What an evening!" Lois whispered to Derek.

"And it's not over yet," said Derek, pulling her gently towards him.

FIFTY-SEVEN

WHEN LOIS AND DEREK FINALLY GOT UP TO DRAW THE curtains and see the day already in strong sunlight, with neighbours going by to buy Sunday newspapers from Josie, Gran had been up for an hour or so, and was impatient to clear away breakfast things and get off to church.

"Just as well you're not Roman Catholic, Mother," said Lois, "or else you might feel you should go to confession and own up to dancing the light fandango and celebrating your profit-making enterprise, deceiving buyers into thinking they were shelling out for diamonds and sapphires."

"Don't be ridiculous, Lois," Gran said firmly. "My conscience is as pure as the driven snow. No such horrible thoughts would cross my mind, and Joan is the same. I think all of us had a great time, as I said last night."

"Only teasing, Mum. Derek and I are very proud of what

you both achieved. And as you can see, I am wearing my lovely present. And now you can rest on your laurels and take up knitting."

"You very well know, my dear daughter, knitting is not one of my many skills. Cooking, yes. Polishing, yes. Scrubbing, yes, if I have to. But I leave knitting to Joan. She knits for the army, I reckon. Shapeless garments in a kind of khaki colour. She says they are for her grandchildren, but I couldn't see either of our Doug's little ones wearing them. What are you two doing this morning?"

"It'll be gardening for me," said Derek.

"I might drive over to Brigham to have a chat with Aurora and Milly. I didn't see them last evening, but then it would probably have been a bit painful for them to come," said Lois.

"Especially as we weren't dealing with their jewellery. You'll probably have to explain that, Lois." Derek was not completely happy with Lois's close friendship with Aurora. Now a widow, she was a troubled soul and probably needed professional help to recover. But he knew better than to say so to his independent wife. Her reaction would be to do the opposite, so he kept quiet.

AFTER DEREK HAD GONE OFF TO HIS VEGETABLE GARDEN CARRYing a hoe like a rifle over his shoulder, Lois set off for Brigham. She knew Aurora opened the bakery shop for three hours on a Sunday morning for people collecting their bread. One or two carried on the age-old tradition of bringing in their joint of meat for roasting in the large bread oven, which remained hot for some hours after bread baking. Milly loved this tradition kept alive and said there was nothing as good as the smell of a rib of beef roasting in their oven.

Occasionally, she suggested to her mother that they should charge for this service. Aurora had refused, saying that it cost them nothing, and anyway, she did not offer the service to all comers. There were still hard-up families in the village, and if not starving, they were finding it hard to make ends meet in the current climate of government cuts in welfare.

Milly saw the wisdom of this. If times improved, those they helped would be good customers in the future.

"Morning, Lois!" Aurora was beaming, and wrapped up Lois's bread with expert fingers. "I hear it all went very well last evening. Congratulations to Gran and Joan. I shall have to watch out!"

"Have you decided to keep on your Luxury Jewellery parties?"

"Still not decided. To tell the truth, Lois, I dread it. I never did like selling that stuff, and when I helped out, Donald said I looked so superior I was bad for business. But I wasn't. Superior, I mean. I thought the jewellery was overpriced, which, of course, it had to be to make it profitable for several layers of selling. No, I think if I can keep the bakery property and business going, and maybe expand a little on the cake side, I shall be able to keep Milly and me until she gets a job and becomes independent. My wants are small, and all I ask is to be able to sit on the wall of the millpond and look at the ducks and think how lucky I am."

Lois smiled encouragingly, but was puzzled. Surely all

Aurora wanted was her husband back again, and Milly a qualified nurse, with perhaps a nice boyfriend and a wedding in the offing. But no, perhaps not her husband back again.

She shrugged and smiled at Aurora. "You're a good, brave person," she said. "And going to ground in your hideaway obviously gave you time to do some constructive thinking."

Aurora looked at her watch. "Time to shut up shop," she said. "Do you fancy a stroll over the meadow, and a drink at the Mill? Did you bring Jemima?"

"That would be nice," said Lois. "Yes, Jeems is in the van, so I'll get her out and meet you by the pond, okay?"

"We might see Milly, on her way back from church. My daughter has fallen in with a church youth group since she's been at home. Nice youngsters they are, too. But I always feel somehow sinful when they are around!"

"You know what Gran would say! 'Let he who is without sin cast the first stone.' Not that I am suggesting your youngsters are casting stones! But you know what I mean."

"Depends on the magnitude of the sin, I suppose," said Aurora, a half smile of gratitude on her face. "You are a good friend, Lois, and I'm not sure if I could have surfaced at all without our friendship."

"Before we get bogged down on a graded list of sins, I'll go and get Jeems!"

THE WATER MEADOW BESIDE THE MILL WAS FULL OF STROLLERS, some with dogs on long leads and others with babies in backpacks. There was a lovely atmosphere of peace and joy, thought Lois. Difficult to believe that such a horrible death as that of Donald Black had happened in the green water driving the old mill wheel. If the workmen had replaced the safety panels, this would be perfect. So thought Lois. She and Aurora sat outside with Jeems, drinking glasses of cider and sharing a packet of crisps.

"I've been thinking, Lois, and I'd appreciate your opinion. I've always supplied bread and rolls and that sort of thing to the Mill kitchens, but now I thought I would expand into catering on a larger scale. Not taking over from them, but offering to do roasts and pies, and helping out when they have big receptions and so on. What do you think?"

"I think it's a great idea! You've got just the right setup for that. And you have only yourself to please. I'd drop the jewellery idea and concentrate on something you love to do."

"That's exactly how I look at it. Wonderful! Can I buy you another cider to celebrate?"

Lois thought that a celebration was perhaps a little premature. Aurora seemed to have shut the door on past terrors, and set off again in a different direction. Which was fine and sensible, but Lois found it a little uncomfortable, and said she had to get back to escape the wrath of Gran, who was decidedly uppity after yesterday's success.

FIFTY-EIGHT

❧

"I'LL JUST NIP INTO THE LADIES' ROOM," SAID AURORA, "WHILE you take Jeems to the car. And then I'll meet you back at the bakery, so's you can pick up your bread. Shan't be two ticks."

Jeems protested about being shut up in the car, whining in a heartbreaking howl. It took Lois several minutes to placate her with a couple of biscuits and a promise that she would be back directly.

Aurora, meanwhile, was in the ladies' room glad of the hotel amenities, which she often used instead of her own, upstairs and very chilly in wintertime. Now she came out into the backyard, surrounded by a high brick wall, only to find her way barred by a small, weaselly-looking character with his cap pulled down over his eyes.

"Excuse me," she said politely. "I need to come out this way to get to my bakery shop."

He didn't answer, and remained standing in her way. She was about to turn and go back into the hotel to find another exit, when he spoke.

"I seen 'im. I saw 'im the day he went into the water. An' I saw several other things. It'd be worth your while to help me out with a tenner, and I could forget what I saw happen then."

Aurora stared at him. "I have no idea what you are talking about," she said. "If you don't go away and leave me alone, I shall call for the police. There's always one patrols round here about now."

"You'll regret it, Mrs. Black. But I am always up the road in the hostel. You can find me there."

Aurora was growing angry. "I have no intention of finding you again, ever. So get out of my way, and let me pass! My friend is waiting, and she's got a very bad-tempered terrier."

"Ha! It'll take more than a bloody dog to scare me. Anyway, I've said what I got to say, and I'll wait for you to contact me. Up the road. The White House hostel, for tramps like me."

He vanished quickly, so quickly that Aurora did not see where he went, but it certainly wasn't the gate in the wall, where she went quickly and found Lois waiting for her.

"Who was that funny little man?" Lois asked. "He passed me, going like a bat out of hell, muttering to himself."

"Oh, poor little so-and-so. It was probably one of the

alkies from the hostel at the top of the road. Most of them have rotted their brains with drinking. Poor souls. People round here have tried to get them moved somewhere else, but the authorities have refused. I sometimes give them a bun and a cup of coffee if they are sitting on the pond wall. They are always polite and grateful, but this one had rather alarmingly claimed to have seen Donald fall. He was insinuating nasty things, and I don't intend to worry about him and his lies."

Not worrying will not be that easy with the nasty piece of work who challenged me just now, Aurora thought to herself. I shall have to be careful to stay out of his way. I do hope he wasn't told to clear off by Donald that morning. Donald was one of the people trying to get rid of the residents of the White House, which he said gave the area a bad name. Weaselly man was so sure I would have something to hide, the idiot. I didn't give him money, though. I've never given any of them money. The staff up there did not encourage it.

She realised Lois had said something to her but she had no idea what. She was shaking and felt she wanted to tell Lois about the nastiness of the man's sudden unexpected threat. Lois was duly sympathetic, and said all the right comforting things.

But "Odd," Lois said to Jeems, who had settled on her bed in the back of the van. "Very odd indeed."

MILLY HAD RISEN LATE, BUT WHEN SHE SAW HER MOTHER AND Lois Meade with a dog over the meadows, she decided to tidy the bakery and put the stale loaves under the counter in plastic bags. They were fine for the ducks, and several families came out regularly on Sunday afternoons with children who loved to feed the birds. It had been Milly's idea to sell stale bread for a few pennies, and she enjoyed talking to the young families. She loved the babies especially, and was hoping to specialise in paediatrics when she went back to the hospital.

"Hi Mum," she said now, as Aurora came into the bakehouse. "Did you have a nice morning with Mrs. Meade?"

Aurora nodded. "Yes, we had a lovely time. There was a slight hitch when we came back. Lois went to put Jeems in the car, and I went to the loo in the hotel, like I often do. Then when I came out, there was this little man in a tweed cap waiting for me. Tried blackmail! Some trumped-up story about your father and the Mill. I sent him packing, not very kindly, I'm afraid. Never give in to blackmail, Milly, and if he accosts you, walk right past him."

"Was he from the White House?" said Milly.

"He said so. I've never seen him before. They have quite a quick turnover up there. Some of those far-gone residents don't last long, poor things."

"Well, never mind about the inhabitants of the White House; why don't we treat ourselves and have lunch in the bar restaurant over the road?"

"Good idea," said Aurora. "A couple more glasses of cider, and I shall be anybody's!"

Milly laughed, but covered her surprise at her mother's answer. She looked at her, her cheeks pink and eyes sparkling at the idea of being anybody's. Of course, Milly thought, her mother was a relatively young woman, and very attractive in her efficient way. Extraordinary, really, that she could not remember a single occasion when her father had made any affectionate gestures, or even gave any indication that he still fancied her.

But then again, Aurora was very cool. Pleasant and fond of her only child. But cool. That couldn't be said for her father with other women. Some of those who came over from the hotel to buy bread were all over him, and he clearly enjoyed it!

So where does that leave me? Milly thought. A bit of Mum's inherited genes, I expect. Best not to think too much about it.

FIFTY-NINE

ॐ

Today was Monday, and Lois sat in her office preparing for the midday meeting of her team. She found she was moving the same piece of paper from one side of her desk to another, while her mind was on other things.

Yesterday's walk with Aurora and her story of the tramp's attempt to blackmail her had alarmed Lois. It could have been a weak attempt to grab a small amount of money for drink, or the weasel might have been after bigger rewards. Aurora seemed to be taking it reasonably lightly, but when she handed Lois an extra free loaf only just out of date, her hands were shaking.

The obvious thing was for either Aurora herself, or Lois on her behalf, to inform Inspector Cowgill. It would be easy enough for the inspector to visit the White House with Aurora and identify the weasel. A Monday morning was perhaps not a good idea, but maybe after the team meeting, she would give him a ring and judge his reaction. She supposed the police were well acquainted with the residents of the White House, mainly concerned with petty crime. But occasionally, surely, they must have had to investigate more serious matters. And what was this one? Something to do with the death of Aurora's husband, Donald, and of his fancy woman in the hotel? A witness?

Lois picked up her phone and dialled Aurora.

"Hi, Lois! How are you this morning? That was a lovely walk we had yesterday. Thank you so much for winkling me out to take dear little Jeems across the meadows."

"Yes, it was fun. Except for your encounter with a threatening, weaselly man. That is partly why I am ringing. How would you feel about telling Cowgill what you've told me? He could probably give the nasty unfortunate a stern warning and tell him to keep out of your way. What do you think?"

Aurora's voice changed. "No, Lois. I don't need that," she said in a bright, firm tone. "Those men in the White House have enough to put up with, usually to do with the killer diet of the down-and-out. And I have good relations with the people at the White House. They trust me, and I would not lose that for all the tea in China. I will deal with it; don't worry. And in my own way. But thanks for your concern."

Lois was taken aback. She had not previously heard Aurora speaking in such a stern voice, and she couldn't think of anything to persuade her to accept help. They talked of mundane everyday things, and finally Lois said she had to go to prepare for her team meeting.

"And I don't have to ask you," said Aurora, "not to mention all that stuff about my assignation with a weasel! I am quite serious about this, and I know that I can trust you."

Lois shrugged. She could see Dot Nimmo approaching up the garden path. "Hardly an assignation," she said, and signed off.

THE MEETING BEGAN WITH LOIS CALLING THE GOSSIPS TO ORDER. "Quiet, you lot," she said, smiling. "Let's have complaints first of all. Any dissatisfied customers? You first, Dot."

Dot smiled blandly. "All my clients are more than satisfied," she said.

"And you, Floss? How are you coping with Mrs. Prentise?"

"Not bad. She is a bit stuffy sometimes, but spends most of her life on the telephone to her friends. At least, I suppose they are friends. One of them seems to be that Aurora Black. Very chummy, they are."

"Bearing in mind that one of our basic rules is never to eavesdrop deliberately on clients' private conversations, was there anything else you could not help hearing? Anything of interest to this meeting?"

Floss could hear the encouragement in Lois's voice, and shook her head. "Only that they were gossiping in reception in the hotel. The cleaners, I mean. Discussing Joan and Gran's next jewellery party in the hotel."

"*What* did you say? Another jewellery party?" said Lois.

"Yes, they were all excited about it. Should do well."

"There was one other thing," added Floss. "You know that Gloria? The one with the fancy bedroom in her mother's house? Well, her name was mentioned more than once.

Seems she has been interviewed by the police a couple of times recently. I thought you'd be interested, Mrs. M."

"Thanks, Floss. Now, remind me to have a word with my mother. Jewellery parties indeed! But let's change the subject. As you know, I am most anxious to find out who pushed Donald Black into the water. If he *was* pushed. He could have fallen or, most unlikely, jumped. It has been a very distressing time for my friend Aurora, and it would be good to have the whole thing cleared up. Thank you for your input, Dot and Floss. Now let's get on. Andrew, anything to report?"

Andrew said that his two jobs, redecorating the hotel and occasional cleaning when the staff was extra busy, were turning out to be very interesting. "Bearing in mind," he said, with a small smile, "that we never deliberately eavesdrop on clients' conversations, it is sometimes difficult for me to avoid that. Sometimes I think I'm invisible with a paintbrush in my hand. Unfortunately, I don't know many of the hotel's visitors. There's constant coming and going, of course. What's more, I am not particularly interested in them, unless something stands out from the norm."

"I used to love 'im," said Dot.

"Who?" Andrew frowned.

"Norm. Little Norm. Norman Wisdom, o'course. He was great on the telly!"

"On which note," said Lois. "I hereby close the meeting."

SIXTY

❧

WHEN THEY HAD ALL GONE, GRAN CAME IN WITH A question. "What was so funny? I could hear them laughing from up the garden in among the bean sticks!"

"It was your favourite person made us laugh, Mum. Dot Nimmo can be very funny at times. Anyway, are we having runners for lunch? Lamb chops and runner beans. Very restoring. What would we do without you?"

"Very well, I should think."

"Forget it, Mum. Now, I have to go into town this afternoon. An appointment at three. And before you ask, yes, it is to see the inspector."

"Thanks for telling us," said Gran sourly. "Lunch is nearly ready, you'll be pleased to know, and Derek is coming up the drive."

*   *   *

LOIS RETURNED AURORA'S CALL AND INVITED HER TO COME TO tea at about five o'clock. Hot buttered toast and honey, she said, and Aurora cheered up immediately.

"And best not to mention parties, Mum," Lois said, alerting Gran to the guest for tea.

"All right. But if she mentions it first, I'll offer her a job."

"Mum! What do you mean? You told me the Prentise party was the last, and now I hear you're fixing up one with the Mill House Hotel!"

"Did I say that?" said Gran. "Well, you never know, do you, how things will turn out? After all, when we moved here from Tresham, you had no intention of ferretin'. Too much to do with three children, if I remember rightly. Anyway, eat your lunch. You won't want to keep the inspector waiting."

Derek came in, shaking his head and saying it was a gale blowing out there, with rain like bullets. "Do you have to go out, Lois?" he said, sitting down at the table. "And are we allowed to know where you are going?"

"To see Cowgill. He wants to ask me some questions."

"Surely he could come here? I mean, what's the use of having a policeman in the family if you can't pull a few strings?"

"I also have to collect my shoes from the menders. Is that a good-enough reason? Now, I'm off. Thanks for lunch, Mum. See you later."

She kissed Derek on the top of his head, collected her handbag and keys and left.

Tresham was busy, and the heavy rain had caused clashes of umbrellas. The police-station car park was full, and Lois found a place on the other side of the street. Then she put her head down and ran through the storm to the station entrance, where the door was thrust open, almost crashing into her face.

"Gloria! Be careful! Hi, don't go!" But Gloria had disappeared into the crowds.

"Good day, Mrs. Meade," said the desk sergeant, "though it isn't, is it? The inspector is expecting you." His wide smile was teasing, and he gestured up the stone stairs.

"Ah, Lois, my dear. Come and sit down. Are you wet? It is a shocking day. Come here and let me help you take off those wet shoes."

"No chance!" said Lois. "Nice try, though. Now, I don't have much time, so shall we make a start?"

Cowgill contented himself with taking out a large, white folded handkerchief and drying the rain from her face, then kissing her lightly on her cold, rosy cheek.

"Right, then shall I begin?" said Lois. "You have not yet given me the result of the postmortem on Sylvia Fountain. I've been mugging up on such things, and it sounds as if the results are divulged only to a close member of the family. Not me, for instance. But my colleague, Gloria Prentise, was a cousin of Sylvia, and from what she has told me, they were more like sisters. Gloria is very upset at Sylvia's horrible death. She swears she is as interested in finding her murderer as I am, but for a different reason. I am concerned only with an attempt to help my friend Aurora Black."

"Whose husband was Sylvia Fountain's lover. I should have thought Gloria would rejoice in getting rid of Donald Black."

"That might be part of it, but I think she feels the whole sordid business needs to be finalised. I don't know what finalised would mean in Prentise circles, though I do know I wouldn't want to be at the rough end of what they consider justice. Now, we want to know the results of the postmortem, as they could well help us to avoid more violence. Revenge killings, an' that. Will you confirm Gloria is close family, and talk to her?"

Cowgill sighed. "I had looked forward to an afternoon with my lovely Lois, but now all I have to tell you is that I gave Gloria the postmortem results before you arrived. You must have seen her leaving."

"Yes, I did, and she did not stop. Oh my Lord, Cowgill! We have to catch her right away to make her stop. Depends what the results were, of course, but if it gave Gloria some really important clues as to who killed Sylvia, I hate to think what she or her family might do. Gloria is an odd person, and not one I would necessarily trust, but we have a pretty fragile truce between us, and I might be able to stop her doing anything silly."

"Stop what exactly?"

"Stop her before she finds the answer to her search, or

thinks she has found the person, and possibly decides to avenge poor strangled Sylvia there and then."

Cowgill stood up. "My dear Lois, aren't you getting a little fanciful? Though I agree that Gloria Prentise was certainly very angry about something, and muttered that she had to get to Brigham straightaway. Mm, well, you're not usually wrong, so come on, my dear," he said, reaching for her wet coat. "I'll order the car, and we'll go back to Long Farnden so that you can change into dry clothes."

"No time. Let's go straight to Brigham. We may be in time, and I'll never speak to you again if we aren't. All my efforts to help Aurora will be in vain."

"Now you're verging on the melodramatic! What on earth are you expecting? Pistols at dawn? We have plenty of time, if so."

"Not so sure about that. And don't come the *humph*ing detective with me. I'll go on my own if you'd rather. C'mon."

SIXTY-ONE

⁂

INSIDE THE BAKERY, AURORA HAD GREETED GLORIA COOLLY, and said she was sorry, but all the bread had gone. She had some bread rolls if they would do instead.

Gloria had replied that she did not want bread or rolls, but an honest and detailed account from Aurora about what exactly happened the night her cousin was killed in the hotel, and who attempted to fudge the real cause of her death.

Now Aurora sat on the edge of a chair in her living room, shaking her head and pale as a ghost. "What makes you think I have answers to those questions?" she said.

"I don't think. I know. I know that the necklace did not strangle poor Sylvia. Either you or your poncey husband strangled her with your hands—though I doubt Donald had the strength. Sylvia was a fit person, and used to dealing with drunks in the Purple Dog."

"All this is absolute nonsense!" Aurora said. "How dare you come in here and accuse me of murdering my husband's lover! And now I have work to do, so I'll thank you to leave. Now, please. Go on, get out!" She stood up and approached Gloria.

"Don't touch me, Aurora Black!" shouted Gloria. "You may be the original Strong Woman, pushing bread dough around in here, but I could deal with you with one blow."

"Very ladylike!" said Aurora, and continued to walk toward the shop door. "Get going, Miss Prentise. I suggest you stay away from my bakery in the future. I am not accustomed to being threatened with lying rubbish in my own home." She paused and stood aside to make way for Gloria to leave.

"Oh my Lord!" said Gloria, stopping in her tracks, and looking out of the window. "See who we have coming to call? Or should I say, to the rescue? They needn't have bothered. I wouldn't have dirtied my hands touching you, Aurora Black! Open the door for them, won't you? And there's your friend from Farnden. Policeman's fancy woman? Your little pal? Let's see if they have stumbled on the truth for once."

ON THEIR WAY TO THE BAKERY, COWGILL HAD TOLD LOIS the results of the postmortem, and they had discussed the possibility of a second person—a dissatisfied customer, maybe?—being involved in the well-planned murder of Sylvia. Someone had hoped to convince whoever found her that the silver necklace had strangled her. Quite clever, Lois had thought. She was actually strangled with gloved hands around her neck, the necklace tightened to breaking point to look like it had done the job. Then she was manhandled fully dressed, into bed, covered up so that anyone walking into the room would think she was asleep.

Yes, really clever, Cowgill had agreed with Lois. But nigh on impossible for one person on his or her own. There must have been two persons, working quickly and efficiently. Very strong, in both body and mind.

"And you think it might have been Gloria?" asked Lois, as they approached Brigham.

"Not sure," said Cowgill. "What do you think?"

"I think you know perfectly well who killed Sylvia Fountain, and are biding your time until that someone gives him- or herself away. Right?"

"Not quite. There is one other piece in the jigsaw. One of the reception staff of the hotel has come forward with a sighting of Donald Black in the hotel that night. Her friend told her to report it, as it might be important, but she has only just done so. Terrified of the police, apparently. A pleasant woman, but not the brightest. She hadn't thought anything much of it, as they were all used to seeing him around."

"What? In the middle of the night?"

"Especially in the middle of the night, tapping at Sylvia Fountain's bedroom door. Here we are, my dear. Let's go straight in."

SIXTY-TWO

✦

"How convenient," said Gloria sourly. "Quite a jolly little meeting, eh?"

"Not premeditated, I assure you, and please, Miss Prentise, stay with us for a little longer. But if you were thinking of making a run for it, I do have chaps stationed outside," said Cowgill. "Now, as we are here together, perhaps I may ask Mrs. Black if she minds us looking for a few answers to questions I need to ask."

"I don't suppose I have a real option, do I, Inspector? Please sit down, anyway, and I hope it won't take too long. I have to meet Milly from a train in Tresham shortly. She has had a day in London with her friends from the hospital."

"Bless her," said Lois. "Might be a good thing. Carry on, Inspector. We're all ears."

"First of all, I think I may assume that we all want to

find the person who killed Sylvia Fountain in such a brutal and calculated way. She was throttled by strong hands and had a silver necklace tightened around her throat in an attempt to hide the real cause of death. The fact that it was a necklace from the Brigham Luxury Jewellery collection is not accidental. It was meant to point to one person."

"But why kill my Sylvia?" said Gloria. "I can tell you truthfully, Inspector, that Sylvia was the kindest, most peace-loving person I know—knew."

"It is a myth, I know," said Cowgill, "that prostitutes are supposed to have hearts of gold, but in my experience, they need to be tough and sometimes ruthless. It is a dangerous profession. Now, question number one. It has emerged that Donald Black was seen in the hotel on the night of Sylvia's murder."

"Don't be ridiculous," said Lois. "He may have been in the hotel, but it doesn't mean he attacked Sylvia. Aurora, you wouldn't think him capable of that, would you?"

"Um, well," she replied, colour rising in her face. "I'm not sure, Lois. He was quite proud of looking fit and trim. He used to work out quite often. Good for business, he used to say, if I ever queried his spending a fortune on tittivating. So yes, he was wiry and strong."

"Question number two," said Cowgill. "Where were you that night, Mrs. Black? I know we have had your statement already, but indulge me."

"Best to answer the inspector, Aurora," said Lois.

"I have no intention of indulging you, Inspector, or my erstwhile friend here, Lois Meade. I was in bed asleep. I think I heard Donald's bedroom door shut at some point, but I didn't look at the clock. I expect he'd got out for a pee."

"Question number three." Cowgill smiled at them, as if in triumph. "At what time did you follow him, Mrs. Black, over to the hotel, finding him in the arms of one Sylvia Fountain?"

"What? Of course I didn't follow him! I won't deny that I hadn't thought of it from time to time. He has tortured me for so long, humiliated me in front of others, but I had no wish to see my husband in flagrante delicto with a blonde whore."

"There you are, then," said Gloria, glaring at Cowgill. "The wicked sod killed Sylvia, his lover who had been so accommodating to him. She was a big girl. Very able and pleasant."

"That's probably why he liked her at first," said Aurora. "Donald was quite short for a man, although he was quite handsome, some said. She probably made him feel tall, don't you reckon, Miss Prentise? You are the expert on these things."

"No need to be narky, Aurora Black," said Gloria. "Now, Cowgill, what's question four?"

"This one is for you. Did you talk to your cousin about the Blacks? Did you have any idea that there was big trouble brewing?"

"Oh yes. Donald was insisting Sylvia ministered to him alone. No other customers allowed. He had already told her she was the sole beneficiary in his will. He said he would pay her extra, but she was unwilling. She said he could be quite difficult at times, and she had no wish to be only his client. She told me lately that he had started saying he would leave his wife and marry her. But Sylvia was not keen, and in any case did not really believe him. He was very angry, she said, and she was in a quandary as to what she should do."

"So you helped her to make up her mind?"

"No, Inspector. She decided herself. She was going to tell him to bog off and leave her alone. No more assignations."

"Ah," said Aurora. "That explains it."

"Explains what, Mrs. Black?" Cowgill was beginning to wonder whether he should abandon the group therapy and question them singly.

"Explains why he was in such a foul mood that day. All day, he was."

"Question number five: did he throw himself into the water at the Mill in remorse, do you think, Mrs. Black?"

"I haven't said I think he had anything to regret. I wasn't there, and knew nothing more than that he may have gone out at night. I went back to sleep. And yes, I was so used to his little ways that I made no comments next day and let him get on with it."

"With what?" said Lois. "With falling into the water? With cracking his skull on the concrete edge? You were pretty cut up when you heard what had happened to Sylvia, and maybe saw your husband as her attacker?"

Aurora stared at her. "Lois! How could you? Of course I was. I never wished her dead. But nor did I want her as my best friend."

Cowgill pounced. "So weren't you quite pleased when you heard your problems with Sylvia Fountain were solved in a way that had nothing to do with you? Exit Sylvia Fountain?"

"What are you suggesting?" said Lois. "That Sylvia and Donald were varying the fun and inadvertently caused her death? It happens. For God's sake, Cowgill, wind this up and let us go home."

Lois was red in the face with frustration. She had come to her own conclusion and was sure she could work it all out in detail if she could talk privately with Aurora.

Cowgill stared at her. "Very well, Lois. I shall be questioning you further one by one, and I hope we shall have some success. Thank you for your time today, ladies. It has been most useful. Don't any of you leave town without telling me. Good day all."

And he stood up, turned on his heel, and left them openmouthed with surprise.

SIXTY-THREE

❧

NEXT MORNING, LOIS WALKED DOWN TO THE SHOP TO fetch the papers and buy milk. She fancied going for a walk with Jemima to clear her head. Last evening's events had left her muddled and unsure where the truth lay.

As always, Josie's shop had become the centre of attention, especially as Lois walked in. Silence fell, and Josie laughed. "Morning, Mum. What can I get you? The baker has left some freshly made cakes, if you fancy one. Or doesn't our Gran allow you to buy cakes?"

"The papers, please, and a bottle of milk. But I don't mind waiting. These ladies were here first."

The ladies, gossips all, melted away slowly, their business finished, and Lois sat down on the stool by the counter. "That was well done, Josie love," she said. "I'm glad to have some time to think."

"It's Aurora, isn't it? You are worried about how she's going to face up to all this. But I wouldn't worry. She's quite a tough lady, I reckon. And Milly will help. What are you up to today? I diagnose depression, and think you should go for a nice long walk with Jemima."

"You've read my mind. I am going to do just that. And, by the way, if you hear anything useful about Donald Black, let me know."

"Forget it, Mum! The man was a pain in the bum, and won't be much missed. Aurora will need your support, so concentrate on her. That's my advice."

THE MEADOWS BY THE RIVER WERE COOL AND DAMP, AND LOIS walked uncaring through long, wet grass and squelchy moss as she threw Jemima's ball for her and extricated her from the marshy bits. Reaching dry ground, she quickened her step and headed for the little bridge that led back to the village and home.

"Come on, Jeems," Lois said, when they were both muddy and cold and had wet feet. "Let's go and find Gran."

GRAN HAD MADE COFFEE FOR HERSELF AND LOIS, AND WAS looking forward to a quiet chat to see if her daughter would unburden herself and stop looking so worried. But as she was about to sit down, a shadow passed the kitchen window, and then there was a light tap at the door.

Lois, already sitting at the table, sighed. "It's Aurora, Mum. Could you let her in? Is there enough coffee?"

"I have a good mind to say we are busy and can she come back later! But I suppose you wouldn't want that."

"No, quite right. Let her in."

Aurora attempted a smile. "Sorry to interrupt, Lois, but I wondered if you can spare me a few minutes' chat."

Lois did not answer. She thought she was sure that it was going to take a lot more than a few minutes. "Of course, Aurora. Come and sit down," she said finally.

"If you don't mind, Lois, I'll take my coffee through to the sitting room," said Gran. "It's my favourite antiques auction programme on the box."

"Oh, am I driving you away?" said Aurora.

Lois was tempted to answer yes, she was, but she held her tongue. When Gran had left them, Lois looked straight at Aurora and said, "Right, now let's have the truth. What exactly did happen the night of Sylvia's murder? We have been pussyfooting around for long enough. Whose idea was it? Yours or Donald's?"

Aurora stared at her. Then she began to get up from her chair.

"Sit down!" said Lois. "You came here to tell me the truth, I hope, and ask for my help. The best thing I can do for you is to hear you through an account of exactly what happened. And, if necessary, why it happened."

"And then you promise to help me?"

"If I can, of course I will. Now, when did you tackle Donald? He was threatening to leave, to go and live with Sylvia, and maybe changing his will to make her sole beneficiary. Am I guessing right? But she wouldn't have him, and he didn't believe her. Am I right?"

Aurora nodded. "He taunted me, saying I had no idea how to love him, and Sylvia was more to him than anyone he'd ever met." Tears were streaming down her face, and Lois silently handed her a tissue.

"So you talked about it. Carry on from there. And buck up. You've a lot to get through. Do you want more coffee?"

Aurora shook her head. "It was like a shaft of sunlight through the gloom, Lois. I suddenly saw a clear way out of it. After all, he was threatening to take away *my* life. All our possessions, including the house and bakery, were in his name, and he claimed he had altered his will in Sylvia's favour. I had argued about this, but he always laughed it off, as if it was not important."

"Very convenient. So what was the clear way?"

"That Donald should do the whole thing. He was angry and upset that she had turned him down, and said that if he couldn't have her, he'd make sure no one else did. I did not even mean to go over to the Mill with him. I knew a good way through a back entrance, and would follow to make sure he bullied her to clear out for good. I had a key, anyway, in case I wanted to leave perishables in the hotel fridges."

"Donald was to do the whole thing, but you went over to the Mill with him and it went wrong?"

"He had arranged with a chum up north to sleep in his bed, but leave in the small hours after he had been seen with the covers pulled over his head. Donald told him he had wife trouble. Then, blow me if he didn't bottle out at the last minute! Said he couldn't do it, and was calling the whole thing off. I had planned it carefully, down to the last necklace thing. So anyway, he said he would only do it if I would come with him. It was getting late and dark, and I knew he would never be able to screw himself up to it again, so I said yes, I would help him. We went separately to the Mill, and I think one of the reception staff saw me. She was wandering around, looking for her friend. Donald was outside Sylvia's door, and said he too thought the receptionist had seen him. Not a good start, and it set Donald into blubbing and saying he was going back."

"Blubbing?"

"Yes, he was a terrible coward and cried like a baby if anything serious happened to him. Well, this was serious! Anyway, we got there, and I told him to tap on Sylvia's door. When she opened it, I pushed him through into Sylvia's arms and, much to Miss Fountain's annoyance, I followed."

"She was fully dressed, not ready for bed?" said Lois.

"We had an argument about that. After the accident, I was for undressing her and getting her into bed, so it would look more natural. But Donald refused to undress her. Misplaced sense of decency, I suppose!"

"Carry on, but don't glory in it, else I shall lose what shreds of sympathy I have left for you."

Aurora stared at her. Then she stood up, pushing her chair back with a rasping sound. "If that's how you feel, I won't trouble you any longer. I thought you would give me some advice and help what to do next. But no. I was wrong."

"You are not wrong. Please sit down, Aurora. It is not easy for me to listen to details such as these, from my good friend and companion in walks with my dog over the water meadows. If it helps you, I am ready to listen. I don't have to tell you what will happen next. Do I?"

Aurora shook her head. "So shall I carry on? I would rather you had it straight, rather than some garbled version cobbled together by the police."

Lois managed a smile. "I think we can trust Inspector Cowgill to get it right," she said.

"With your help," said Aurora. "Shall I carry on?"

"So she pushed you out, or tried to?"

"Yes, she was holding a paper knife, or some such, and came at me aiming straight at my face. I grabbed anything I could get hold of, and it was unfortunately her neck. I held it tight with both hands—gloves on—until she dropped the knife, and then I squeezed to make sure she had given up. I did not mean to strangle her, I swear to that, Lois. It was self-defence, however you look at it."

"It'll be Cowgill you'll have to convince, but I must say you went to extraordinary lengths to disarm her. What was Donald doing all this time?"

"Blubbing, as I said. He got between me and the door, so I couldn't escape from Sylvia. It was me or her, in the end."

"Then what?"

"When we realised she'd stopped breathing, I had to take charge, and came up with the plan. Get her into bed, and make it look as if she had been strangled with the silver necklace. Donald was in such a mess that he didn't realise I had gloves on, and he hadn't. Lucky for me!"

"And next morning, did you discuss it over your toast and marmalade?"

"Lois! Please! You asked me to give you an accurate account, and I have. But there is one thing more. I was aware of the shocking thing we had done, and terrified what would happen when someone found Sylvia. And then, and then . . . I am not asking you to keep this to yourself, because I know you wouldn't do anything so wicked. But I hope you will tell it straight to Cowgill."

"There's this other thing, isn't there?" said Lois "You made sure you left no fingerprints, but Donald did. Right? And you were hoping against hope that nobody saw *you* either going into the hotel or leaving it. You were rightly guessing that suspicion would immediately fall on him. And you wanted him gone. Gone away from you for ever. No more humiliation, no dishonest scams, defrauding innocent people. No more Donald Black, ever."

"Not entirely right," Aurora said, taking another tissue. "He might have got off lightly and then he'd be back. I had never trusted him, and had no reason to trust him in the future. When I went to the Mill toilet that day we'd had a walk, he was standing in the yard looking down into the water. He shouldn't have been so close, but workmen had moved the safety barriers usually making it impossible for accidents to happen. It was so easy. I had soft shoes on, and he did not hear me coming. On impulse, I gave him a small push, and he was flailing about, hitting his head on the edge as he went. I ran into the hotel and found you there, waiting with our drinks.

"It was a terrible shock when he came in sight spread-eagled on the mill wheel! I thought for a minute that he was alive, but it was just the movement of the water. And the rest you know, Lois."

To Lois's relief, Aurora got up from the table and walked toward the kitchen door. She sniffed, and with a choked "Goodbye," left.

Sixty-Four

～

"COWGILL? IS THAT YOU?"

"Yes, Lois, it is me. And I am on my way to see Mrs. Black. She has telephoned and asked to see me. I suggested I come to her, and, if you wish it, you may be there to support her."

"Thanks, Cowgill. You may not think me much of a friend, but I think she will be better with you by herself. She is a very strong character, and has given me a very clear account of what happened that night. Now she has to do the same for you. There may be other times when she needs my support, when I shall willingly give it. Is that sensible, d'you think?"

"I shall need to check with you her statement in detail, but for the immediate future, I think perhaps you should not see her. I shall be taking her into custody in any case.

Will you be able to help Milly? It is going to be a terrible shock for her, and we must minimise it as much as possible."

"Josie will be able to help there. They have become pals since we were introduced to Milly, so I am sure there will be a lot we can do to help. What a dreadful case, Hunter. I am strongly tempted to call it a day. No more ferretin'. Think how happy Derek would be. What do you think?"

"I think you should do what your heart tells you, Lois. With your Josie married to my nephew Matthew, we shall meet on occasions. I could not bear to think we would never see each other again. Officially, of course! Bless you, my love. I know you will come to the right decision. And now I must go and be very official with Aurora Black."

EPILOGUE

❦

THE BRIGHAM BAKERY WAS UNDERGOING A FRESH COAT OF paint, with the name Milly Black painted in gold on the door. This was underneath the logo of a first-class award in a local competition for a good crusty loaf.

"Hi, Lois," said Milly, as she climbed down the ladder. "Is this too showy, d'you think? Now the place is all mine, I am feeling keen to make it look its best. Wasn't it a turn-up that Dad left me everything in his will? I expect I would be back nursing sick souls if he hadn't. I think I've inherited poor Mum's love of baking. Do you think she will be allowed to bake bread for the other prisoners?"

"'Nuff said about that, Milly. But today I am not too happy to see you up on that ladder without a safety helmet! Can you take a break?"

Milly climbed down, and they went into the shop. "Coffee?" she said. "Oh damn, who's this coming in?"

"Cowgill," said Lois. "Better offer him a cup. Everything has been cleared up now, but it is always a good thing to stay on the right side of the law."

"Sorry—against the rules," said Cowgill, refusing the offer. "But I might accept a muffin in a paper bag, to eat later? Thanks, Milly. Congratulations, anyway, on your award. As far as I am concerned, it is not only for bread, but for bravery, too! Well done, girl. Now, I hoped to find Lois here. Something has come up that might interest you, my dear. There's this derelict house—once a posh job with servants and so on—and a prospective buyer has found something extremely nasty in the attic."

"I don't see how that could possibly interest me," said Lois, smiling at him. "But tell me more."